CAGING LIBERTY

LIBERATING DECEIT BOOK ONE

NICOLE CYPHER

Edited by
KIM BOOKJUNKIE

Copyright © 2023 by Nicole Cypher

All rights reserved.

No part of this book may be reproduced in any form or by any electronic or mechanical means, including information storage and retrieval systems, without written permission from the author, except for the use of brief quotations in a book review.

❀ Created with Vellum

ALSO BY NICOLE CYPHER

For a comprehensive list, check out Nicole's website

The Darker Places Series:

DESIRED

DEPLORABLE

DETHRONED

DEMOLISHED

JULIUS

Soulless Kings MC:

FENDER

JOKER

Gruco Crime Family Series:

HIS PROMISE

HIS PET

HIS PRIZE

HIS PUPPET

HIS PROPERTY

HIS PASSEROTTA (Coming December 2023!)

Liberating Deceit:

CAGING LIBERTY

TAMING LIBERTY

CLAIMING LIBERTY

Standalone Novels:

UNHINGED

VICIOUS KNIGHT

1

———

ANGEL

 y eyes close as I breathe in the cool night air.
If there's one thing I love about New York City, it's the atmosphere. Crisp. Cool... With the sound of traffic and the office lights that act as stars.

It's a change of pace from my usual life that I find peaceful. Like an escape from paradise, something only those who live on a sunny coast could ever understand. The constantly warm sun and salty, moist air can get old.

I open my eyes and lean over the stone railing to watch the people forty stories below shuffle like ants. The charity event my business partner dragged me to is being held on the top floor of who-knows-what-building, and it's currently taking place behind me with only a set of double doors separating the grand hall full of guests from the balcony. The doors were open when I walked out here, but with a kick of the stopper, I'm left alone.

I push myself away from the railing and roll my neck. My hands tuck into my slacks' pockets, and I feel the sleek metal of the cigarette holder I've carried with me for a year. I quit smoking, but I still carry the holder with one lonely cigarette and a lighter inside. It's probably nothing more than a masochistic game I play with myself, but I like to think of it as mastering temptation. I'm stronger for it … and at the same time, weaker.

I open the cigarette case, still in my pocket, then roll the cancer stick between my fingertips, thinking about how good the smoke would feel in my lungs. Blowing out my nose.

I pull the cigarette out and study it pinched between my fingertips.

My jaw clenches as the door behind me opens. I turn to face the intruder, intent on telling whoever it is to leave, but the woman rushes to the ledge several steps away from me and leans over while she tries to catch her breath.

My head tilts and jaw relaxes as I watch her back quake and take in her heavy breathing. The ruby red dress she's wearing extends to her ankles while still showing plenty of skin. It's backless and has a slit up the side that provides a nice, teasing view of her thighs.

Her brunette hair is pinned up, and a pair of diamond earrings dangle halfway down her neck.

My annoyance fades, and I glance through the open doors. Noise filters onto the balcony, and I consider closing the doors, but the click of the woman's heels draws my attention back to her. She steps out of the stilettos, her bottom lip clamped between her teeth as her breathing returns to normal.

"Are you all right?" I ask, staring at her curiously.

She startles and snaps her head to face me, her hand flying to her chest. Our eyes meet, and the blue of her irises pulls me in. The color reminds me of the ocean view from my bedroom balcony, only on her, it's like I'm seeing it for the first time.

I'm struck for a moment, but she's too startled to notice.

She lets out a humored sigh and lifts her red-painted lips into a smile. "You scared me."

"I'm sorry," I say because it sounds appropriate.

"No." She swats to brush away my apology. "I just didn't see you there."

"You seemed preoccupied."

Her polite smile falls, and she brushes a stray strand of hair out of her eyes. She chuckles and paints the smile back on. "Right. I, uh..." She pauses to take a breath. "I just needed some air."

"Were you having a panic attack?" I rest my forearm on the railing and casually lean against it while planting one shoe in front of the other.

She squares her shoulders and shakes her head. My lips tug at the lie I suspect is coming.

"Of course not. Like I said, I just needed some fresh air. It's stuffy in there."

I raise my brows and slowly nod. "I can agree." I allow my eyes to trail down her body for a moment. She's easily the most beautiful woman here tonight.

When I bring my gaze back to her face, she's glaring.

"Right," she deadpans, tugging her dress up to cover spilled cleavage.

"You're not used to these events, are you?" Looking her over, I already know the answer. The women who belong at these things walk with their shoulders back and their noses tilted toward the ceiling. They have smiles plastered on and laugh at almost anything. This woman is trying, and her shoulders are certainly squared, but she doesn't belong here, and she knows it. Thus, the panic attack.

Is she a hooker?

I allow myself another look, then brace for her wrath. She has the body of an upscale escort. One I'd personally pay top dollar for.

When I meet her eyes, her glare has deepened.

I force a frown. "I'm sorry, I don't mean to offend you. I only ask because your dress is a little crooked. You look uncomfortable."

She blinks and looks down. "Oh." She straightens her dress—which was perfectly fine, by the way—and laughs before running her hands over her face. When she drops them at her sides, her shoulders sag.

"This isn't exactly my crowd."

"No?"

She shakes her head.

I guessed as much.

So … not a wife. She looks too young to be a wife anyway. Early twenties probably. I take a peek at her ring finger just to be sure.

She gestures at the railing where my arm rests. "Could I bum one of those?"

"What?"

"The cigarette," she says, gesturing again. "Could I have one?"

I stand up straight and glance at the smoke. It feels wrong to get rid of after all this time, like saying goodbye to a toxic friend, but I suppose it's more a prisoner than anything. Reluctantly, I hand it over, setting my small piece of temptation free. "Sure."

"Thanks." She takes it and brings it to her mouth, leaning forward as I strike the lighter and hover the flame over the tip of the cigarette. She sucks in, and I stare at the orange glow, my senses firing. I set the lighter on the railing and take a step back, watching as the woman takes a drag then breathes out the smoke. I close my eyes for a second, and although it's been a year, I can still taste the nicotine.

"Fuck, I needed that," she says, letting her head fall back

and exhaling. She laughs and straightens her neck, meeting my eyes. "I have no idea what I'm doing here."

"Little out of your league?"

She shrugs and takes another pull before blowing the smoke out through her nostrils. My mouth waters.

"I don't know if I'd put it like that."

"How would you put it?"

She glances inside then meets my gaze. "Rich people are judgmental as fuck."

My lips lift into an amused grin, and I withhold the chuckle creeping up my throat. "You don't say?"

"Seriously, what is even the point of this thing?" She gestures inside. "I mean, how necessary is it to spend all this money throwing a party? Couldn't they have just donated the money they would've spent on their ice sculpture to ALS directly? Do they *need* the tablecloths that cost more than my tuition?"

If I had a dollar for every time I heard that argument, I could have paid for the party myself.

"Tuition?" I ask, my head tilting.

She closes her mouth, stopping herself from saying more, and nods. "Yeah, I'm in law school."

That's interesting.

Daughter, maybe?

No, that doesn't make sense. She obviously doesn't come from money.

She brings the cigarette to her mouth, then lowers it as her gaze drops to my hand. "I didn't take your last one, did I?"

I shrug. "It's fine."

She holds it out to me. "Shit, sorry. Here, we'll share it."

I wave her off. "I'm good."

One brow raises. "I promise I don't have cooties."

"*Really*, you keep it."

"You're sure?"

I nod and force a smile. Internally, I'm dying.

She looks inside, and I take the opportunity to roam my gaze over her, seeing her as more and more appealing as the seconds tick by. Forget the event, she may be the most beautiful woman I've ever seen.

But even more than that, she's … cute. Young but not naïve. A little sassy. Intelligent *and* resourceful if she's a law student using rich, old guys to pay for law school. I'm guessing.

She seems fun. Fresh. *Tempting.* Even more so than the cigarette.

"Sorry if I offended you, by the way."

I blink and meet her eyes. "For?"

"I'm assuming you're here by choice and don't appreciate my 'rich people suck' babble. I'm really just nervous, and this is how I cope with that. Ignore me."

My eyes lower of their own accord, and I quickly force them back to her face. "No offense taken."

"I'm Lib," she says, holding out her hand while the cigarette burns at her side.

I take her hand and squeeze. "Angel."

"Nice to meet you."

I dip my chin and let go of her, my fingertips brushing her palm as I pull away. "You as well."

After taking a final drag of the cigarette, she stubs it out on the century-old, historical stone. My eyes widen, but I bite my tongue.

She glances toward the grand hall again, and I'm almost certain she's going to head back inside, but her heels stay tipped over on the concrete, and she turns back to me. She's stalling.

Good. I don't want her to leave just yet. This is the most engaged I've been all day. Sitting through meetings and attending parties is a necessary part of my life, but I've practically been sleepwalking for hours.

"Where are you from?" she asks.

I blink. "Pardon?"

"You have an accent."

My lips twitch, and I lean against the railing. "Spain. Madrid, to be exact."

"I thought so." She smiles. "I studied abroad for a semester a couple of years ago. Incredible place."

I nod. "It is. I miss it."

"So do I." She gives me a playful wink, and a shiver crawls up my spine. "What made you move to New York?"

I force my eyes to stay on her face and shuffle my feet an inch in her direction. "I didn't. I'm only visiting."

"Ah." She nods as if that makes sense, for whatever reason.

"I'm enjoying it, though. The women here are interesting."

And outspoken.

Her brows bunch, and she moves closer to me. "How so?"

I glance down at Lib's bare feet and half-heartedly lift a shoulder. I don't have an answer for that. Not one I can give her, at least. Truth be told, it's a rare occurrence for me to hear someone with a pussy speak their mind. It's probably been years. So watching this bare-footed woman put a lipstick-smeared cigarette out on precious architecture after ranting about overindulgence is a breath of fresh air. Kind of like New York City is for me.

Lib bends to stand her stilettos upright while I stare down her dress, blood rushing to my cock.

"Well, I should get back in there," she says, stepping into her heels. "Nice talking to you."

She brushes the hair out of her face, gives me a tight smile, then takes a step toward the door.

I grab her arm impulsively, and she halts, spinning toward me.

I smile apologetically and let go of her arm. I have no idea what to say to her, only that I want her to stay.

"Yes?" She quirks a brow when I don't say anything.

I open my mouth to speak words not yet formed, and I'm saved when Sawyer, my business partner and friend, appears in the doorway accompanied by a middle-aged man with salt and pepper hair.

"There you are," Sawyer says, annoyance evident in his tone. His gaze strays to Lib, and heat immediately ignites in his green eyes.

"Hey, honey," Lib says, her stare pinned on the other man. She bites her lip like she's nervous as he comes up to her.

Honey?

I eye up the guy and try to keep the jealousy at bay.

"You disappeared." He puts his hand on her shoulder. "I was worried."

Who the fuck is he, Richard Gere?

"I just needed some air," Lib replies, her tone higher than it was minutes ago.

The man looks at me, and his strained smile grows. "I see you met Mr. Ramos." He slides past me and wraps his arm around Lib's shoulder possessively.

My brow lifts, and I glance at Sawyer a moment, his leer still pinned on Lib. She notices and shoots him a glare that only makes Sawyer smile.

"Do I know you?" I ask Lib's date, turning my attention back to him.

He removes his arm from Lib to hold his hand out toward me. "Robert Gaumond."

"He came to the island once," Sawyer explains, finally dragging his eyes to me. "I introduced you."

"Island?" Lib asks.

Sawyer snickers as Robert shifts uncomfortably for a moment.

Robert clears his throat. "Mr. Hansley owns a small, private island near Fiji. He was kind enough to invite me to a function there once."

A *function?* That's laughable.

"You're welcome back anytime," Sawyer says, his gaze aimed at Lib. "Feel free to bring your pretty, um..." His gaze lowers, then slowly climb back to her face. "*Date.*"

Her eyes widen as she picks up on his not-so-subtle insinuation, and her cheeks blush. He didn't *say* that she's a prostitute, but everyone here could hear it in his tone.

"Right, I remember now," I interject, my words aimed at Robert before Sawyer has a chance to escalate the anger clearly blooming on Lib's face. "How are you?"

"I'm well, thank you," Robert eagerly responds. "And thank you for keeping my girlfriend company."

Girlfriend? I take in all the gray in the man's hair for a second, purposefully not looking at Sawyer's reaction.

"Sorry if I've stolen her," I tilt my head toward Lib.

He waves it off to show it isn't a big deal, although I can see in his rigid posture that he's uncomfortable.

"I'm happy Sawyer had you tag along on this trip. I was actually hoping to run a few business ideas by you."

"Of course," I nod and glance at Lib. She stares off at nothing, her lips set in a firm line and her jaw clenched.

Robert turns to her and puts his hand on her shoulder. "Darling, could you find Mrs. Ash? She's been hoping to talk to you all evening." There's a hint of condemnation in his tone that Lib must pick up on because her shoulders sag. She's not so feisty with this guy.

She nods and turns to leave, but he touches her arm, and she pauses, looking at him expectantly.

"Don't you want to say goodbye to my colleagues, dear?"

She swallows and looks between me and Sawyer, fire igniting in her eyes. "Bye."

I'm a little taken aback by the shift in temperature toward me, but I get it. Guilty by association.

I turn and glare at Sawyer, but he's too busy suppressing a laugh to notice.

"Pleasure meeting you," he responds.

She meets Robert's eyes, then walks back inside. I watch her as she leaves, expecting her to take the desire coursing through me with her, but it only grows.

"Pretty girl," Sawyer comments, turning back to Robert as Lib leaves our sight.

"Yes, she is. We've been together for six months, and I still struggle to concentrate whenever she's around."

"Do you love her?" he asks.

Robert's eyes widen for a moment like he's surprised by the question, but he recovers and shrugs. "I suppose."

That's a yes. He just isn't man enough to admit it. The bastard is probably *smitten.*

"How much?" he asks.

Robert rears back and narrows his eyes. "What are you getting at?"

Sawyer glances at the entrance like he's trying to eye fuck her memory. I know what he's trying to do, and I have mixed feelings about it.

"I'd be interested in purchasing her for the island if you'd be willing to part ways. We could use someone with her spark." He turns to me. "Hell, she was even able to hold *your* attention."

"She's very attractive," I agree with a nod.

Robert chuckles and rubs the back of his neck with a forced smile. "She's not for sale."

"Are you sure?" Sawyer asks, skepticism clear in his tone. "I'd give you a great deal."

I watch Robert with the same skepticism Sawyer does as he thinks. One thing I've learned being friends with

Sawyer is this: everyone has a price. Everyone. Including Lib.

A jolt of excitement shoots through me at the idea of Lib on the island, and I silently chastise myself for it. She's too spirited to be broken, and that's exactly what Sawyer would do if he got his hands on her. Still… It's tempting.

Robert's eyes flicker like he's considering it, but he gives his head a shake to dismiss the idea. "I'm proposing to her, actually. Soon."

"Oh." I force a smile. "Congratulations."

Sawyer doesn't respond.

Robert lets out a strained laugh, and a few moments tick by while he recovers from passing up the offer. "Marriage is a foreign concept to men like you, I'm sure. Believe me, if I lived on the island, we wouldn't be having this conversation. You're both lucky."

Am I?

I gaze at the entrance again. "So move there."

"I hope to," Robert says, pulling my attention back to him. "One day. I'm hoping you can make me a rich enough man so I can afford it."

He takes the opportunity to change the subject and dives into telling me about the line of surf boards—of all things—he wants to produce but needs the initial startup costs for. I don't know why he would bother bringing this to me. Surf boards are not the kind of thing I invest my time or resources in, but I hear him out anyway.

Sawyer stands with his eyes glazed as we talk, and I watch his gaze occasionally travel toward the door, just as mine does. I'm not the only one Lib has piqued the interest of.

I half-listen to Robert for a good thirty minutes before I shake his hand and agree to do business with him, although I'm unsure why. Well, I am, but it's pathetic, and I don't want to admit to myself that I'm this invested in seeing Lib again.

I shouldn't even entertain the idea.

As I leave, I find Lib's eyes among a crowd. She glares and subtly lifts her middle finger at her side. I zero in on it and get the urge to punch Sawyer in the face.

I glance at Sawyer beside me and see him staring at her as well, and I wonder if it's him she's looking at. She doesn't realize it, but she's fucking up horribly right now, only making herself more appealing to him. And to me.

She may not have a price today, but she will.

They always do.

2

LIBERTY

FIVE YEARS LATER

Saltyshells123: You should leave him.

I stare at the words scrolled across my laptop screen and bite my lip. Three dots pop up as saltyshells types, and I move my fingers to the keyboard, intent on saying something so he won't continue.

He's never outright told me to leave my husband before. Over the past year, my chat buddy and I have exchanged countless messages, talking nearly every day, and I've been able to tell myself through it all that it's been innocent. Maybe a little flirting, a few suggestive statements, but far from anything that could be considered cheating. We found each other on a chat site when we were lonely and needed someone to talk to, and the relationship we've built has been platonic. The only reason I didn't tell my husband was because he wouldn't understand, and it would be wrong to unnecessarily worry him.

Now that illusion is at risk of being shattered.

I quickly type out a reply before he can finish whatever it is he's about to say.

manhattanpeasant: You know that isn't appropriate...

The bubbles disappear, and I let out a sigh of relief. It's short-lived, though. A message pops up moments later.

saltyshells123: He doesn't make you happy.

I chew on my lip and sit up straighter on the couch. My heart rate picks up as I stare intently at the screen.

saltyshells123: I could.

I take a deep breath and slowly type out a reply.

manhattanpeasant: You're married. So am I.

saltyshells123: I know, I'm sorry. It's just ... It feels like the only time I'm happy is when I'm talking to you. I would never want to hurt my wife. It's just a lot sometimes.

I sigh and slowly stab the keys.

manhattanpeasant: I know it is.

And I do know. I don't know saltyshells's name—that's something we've agreed to keep private since our first exchange—but I do know just about everything else. His wife was in a horrible car accident two years ago that left her paralyzed and unresponsive. She can understand what he says, and he thinks she knows what's happening a lot of the time, but she can't say or do anything in return. He works from home and doesn't make enough to pay a full-time nurse, so he's her primary caregiver. As sorry as I am for her, I feel sad for him too.

And while I could never fully comprehend his struggles, I do understand the loneliness. I feel it too. Every single moment of the day that I'm not speaking to saltyshells.

How has my life come to this? I used to be vibrant and strong. I used to love life and wake up every day with an enthusiasm I no longer recognize. Why? Why the fuck did I let this become my life?

I type out a message and hit send before I can think it through.

manhattanpeasant: I'm only happy when I'm talking to you too.

saltyshells123: Yeah?

manhattanpeasant: Yes.

saltyshells123: Then let's meet.

I type out a quick 'That would be inappropriate. What would our spouses think?' response, but my finger hovers over the return key.

Am I actually considering it?

No. I would never cheat on my husband...

Right?

Damn it, saltyshells. Why the fuck are you doing this to me?

I slowly hit the backspace key until all my words are gone, then I start typing.

manhattanpeasant: As friends?

saltyshells123: Is that what you really want?

I pull my hands away from the computer and rub my temples.

No, it isn't what I want, and of course, he knows this. He knows almost every intimate detail about me, far more than my own husband does. My dirty secrets, my insecurities... I've spilled it all to him, and he's spilled it all to me. I *know* him. Better than I know anyone.

As stupid as I know it is, and as guilty as it makes me feel, I'm falling in love with him. I've never seen his face, but I know what's in his heart, and I've stayed awake many nights trying not to wonder what would happen if neither of us were married.

I've known the feelings were there, but I've done my best to never let my thoughts go that far. Hoping he doesn't feel the same connection I feel while secretly hoping he does.

I take several deep breaths, then lower my hands and

stare at the screen. I don't know what to say or do. I know what's right, but what's right doesn't align with what I want.

A door upstairs slams, and footsteps pound on the staircase. I close the laptop and perk up just as Elsie, my husband's niece, comes sprinting into view.

"Mail's here!" she announces with so much enthusiasm it's contagious. She bursts out the front door, and I quickly put my laptop away in my bag.

Elsie reappears with a stack of envelopes in hand, then she hurries to the couch and starts sorting through the mail. I move beside her and scan each envelope as she does.

Elsie is a senior in high school and in the process of applying to college. She's a bright and kind kid, and I'm honored to be her sort-of aunt, although we've only known each other for about a year and a half. Tragically, her mother died of breast cancer last year, and Robert, my husband, is her only known relative. Which I thought was odd considering I hadn't been aware that he had a sister.

Elsie and I took a while to hit it off, mainly because she had a preconceived notion that I was a bimbo trophy wife, and she was a tad judgmental. Once we got over that, we became best friends. She's admitted to me that I feel more like family than her uncle does. Which makes sense. My husband can be cold, and he isn't exactly thrilled to have his only niece here until she graduates. But I try to keep Elsie from knowing that.

She flips to an envelope with Harvard's logo, and I feel the energy in the room shift as soon as she sees it. It's the small envelope. We both know what that means.

I put my hand on her back while she gingerly opens the flap and removes the piece of paper that'll be the source of her insecurity for the near future.

She unfolds it, scans the first few sentences, then lowers the paper to her lap.

"Shit," she mutters, emotion clogging her voice.

I rub her back and try to think of the right words to say. I know the truth… This rejection? This rejection is nothing. It doesn't mean shit. Every senior in high school with a high GPA thinks it does, but the reality is, life is full of heartbreak, and not getting into your first-choice school is only the beginning of a string of failures.

Pessimistic, no?

"I've always thought Yale was the better choice anyway," I say, taking the piece of paper from her hands and setting it on the coffee table.

The first tears slip from Elsie's eyes, and I wrap my arm around her and squeeze. "You're gonna be fine, Els."

"No, I won't," she says, her voice cracking. "How can you even say that?"

"Because there's a long list of schools you're waiting to hear back from, and even if you don't get into those, people who go to state schools still get jobs. Screw Harvard."

"Harvard is the only place I've ever wanted to go. It's my dream."

"You'll have bigger dreams. I promise."

"How can you even say that?" she protests, jerking away from me. "You went to Harvard. How would you have felt if they'd rejected *you*?"

Easy. I would've been crushed. Because back then, I was as naïve as Elsie.

The world's a bitch. Maroon sweater or not.

"I would've dodged a bullet. The cafeteria food sucked. And the dorms…" I cringe like I'm reliving a nightmare. "*Jesus*, you would think for eighteen grand a semester you could get more than a flat rock to sleep on and a roommate who doesn't stab your voodoo doll while you sleep."

Her lips lift into the slightest grin, and I wink.

"You really think Yale is better?" she asks.

I nod. "Blows those Harvard bastards out of the water." I clap her knee. "Seriously, kiddo, you're going to love whatever school you go to. Don't let this set you back, not even for a second."

She nods, but I can tell she just let that go in one ear and out the other. She slowly stands. "I need to study," she says, walking around the couch. "Thanks Lib." She leaves the room, and I frown as I watch her go, knowing study is code for 'cry into my pillow.' She's already been through too much heartbreak for her age. It kills me to see her go through more.

She'll get over it, though. She will. And she'll be stronger for the rejection. Maybe if I had been rejected, I wouldn't have been so damn arrogant. You know what they say. Bigger the pride, the harder the fall.

I've fallen pretty fucking hard.

I leave the pity party before it has a chance to fully take off, and I pick up the mail, glancing through it to see if there's anything for me. An embroidered envelope sticks out to me, and I smooth my hand over the 'RE' lettered design.

There's no return address, but whoever this is from must be wealthy to feel the need to have their envelopes specially made. Fucking rich people.

The front door opens, and I turn my head just as Robert walks inside.

"Hey, honey," I say, turning toward him and lowering the stack of mail. I smile but let it fall when he doesn't return it or even return the greeting. "How was your day?"

"Is that the mail?" He drops his briefcase by the door and shrugs out of his coat as he walks toward me.

"Yeah, Elsie was expecting—"

"How many times do I have to ask you not to look through my mail?" he growls, taking the stack of papers from my hand. "Seriously, how many times?"

My eyes narrow, but I try to keep myself from snapping. "As I was saying, Elsie was expecting a letter from Harvard, so she got it from the mailbox when it arrived. I was just glancing through. I don't know why you have to take it as an invasion of your privacy."

"Christ, Liberty, you never listen." He huffs out a breath, sees the letter I was studying, then looks at me with something in his eyes I don't recognize.

"What?" I ask, glancing at the embroidering.

"Did you look through this?" He holds up the letter.

"What are you talking about? The envelope is sealed. I was just—"

"My work is incredibly delicate, and you know that. Everything sent in my name is for my eyes only."

"Fine," I grit out, holding up my hands in surrender. "I won't, under any circumstances, look through the mail delivered to *our* house."

I fight the urge to roll my eyes and try to remember this is just who Robert is. He's neurotically private about his things, not just the mail, but most things. The housekeeper isn't even allowed to clean his office. He keeps it locked at all times, and only he has the key. I knew these things about him when we got married, but I was stupid enough to assume he'd trust me one day.

He doesn't. He never will. I'm not even sure if he *loves* me anymore... Or if he ever did.

My attention drifts to my laptop, but I keep my eyes on Robert.

I'm going to do it. I'm going to meet saltyshells. Maybe it'll be the biggest mistake of my life, but I can't do this shit forever. Maybe if I have something else for a minute, even if it's just another man's friendship, I'll discover a new appreciation for what I have. Hell, maybe it'll *save* my marriage rather than destroy it. Robert currently doesn't register my existence unless I'm annoying him, so how could we possibly get any worse?

Okay, that sounds like a bad justification.

"Can we *please* move on?" I ask, guilt softening the anger in my voice.

Robert takes a deep inhale and nods. "Yes. Please, let's do that." His lips lift into a slight smile as he closes the distance between us and puts his hand on my shoulder. "I'm sorry, honey. I know my idiosyncrasies can be frustrating."

I shrug. "It's fine," I lie.

"Can I make it up to you? I was thinking we could have dinner at Divine tonight. I already made the reservation."

My heartstrings tug, and just like that, I'm conflicted about saltyshells again.

"That's sweet," I say, meaning it. But as soon as the words leave my mouth, my chest deflates. "I would really love that, but I was thinking we could order in tonight. Maybe from that pizza place Elsie likes. She got a rejection letter from Harvard today, and she could use some cheering up."

Robert's lips form a tight smile, and I brace for a fight, but he nods. "Even better." He pokes my nose, something he does that I absolutely hate. "Call it in and come get me when it's here. I have a few things to do in my office, otherwise I would go with you."

"Sure," I say, not at all surprised that he didn't pretend to care about Elsie's bad news.

He starts toward his office, then pauses and looks over his shoulder.

"Oh, and, sweetheart... Could you pick up my dry cleaning while you're out?"

I nod. "Of course."

"Thanks." He winks, then continues toward his office.

I glance at my laptop bag but don't move to retrieve it. Instead, I grab my purse and walk to the foot of the stairs.

"Els, I'm headed out for a bit," I yell up the steps.

I frown when I get no response. The pizza is a pathetic attempt at making her feel better, so I try to rack my brain for something else, but I come up empty.

I lift my purse onto my shoulder and head out the door.

3

———

LIBERTY

I'm pulled awake by a scream.

Something knocks into my shoulder, and my stomach flips as my body sways. I struggle to open my eyes, and when I do, I'm more confused than I was a second ago.

"Help! Somebody help me!"

The scream is right by my ear this time, and I turn my head to the woman it belongs to. My vision is blurry, so it's hard to make out more than her red, curly hair tickling my forearm.

"Help!"

"Shut. Up," another feminine voice groans. I turn my head the other way to see a woman's jet-black hair. My eyes travel down her black sweater and black shorts before landing on a pair of nearly child-sized combat boots.

I shift my arms and wince as my wrists rub against metal. A pole is at my back, and cuffs binding my hands clink against the pole as I adjust my weight to sit up straighter. I blink slowly to try to fight off the grogginess threatening to pull me under. The only thing stopping me from falling asleep is the redhead's scream in my ear.

"Shut the fuck up," the other woman growls. "We're on a boat, you idiot. All you're going to do is draw their attention."

"What's happening?" the redhead whimpers. "What do they want?"

"I don't know. I forgot to ask when they were hitting me over the head with a mallet."

My head lulls from side to side as I try to focus my vision to make sense of my surroundings. Or any of this. Wherever I am, or *we* are, it's dark. And cramped. There are several wooden crates stacked in front of me and nothing but a wall behind it. When I turn to my right, I spot junk in a corner. Some water jugs, a pair of work boots, a few loose pieces of foil that look like wrappers without labels.

All three of us are cuffed to the same pole with our shoulders touching and our legs sprawled in front of us. I try to look behind me, but my neck protests. I wince.

Was I hit with a mallet too?

My head spins, and my stomach bottoms out again. I feel more like I was drugged than hit. I have a headache, but it isn't concentrated to one spot, more like a whole-body ache. And I can barely think. It's like my mind is firing so slowly, I can feel each nerve impulse conducting through Jell-O.

Think.

Think.

Think.

What the hell is going on?

No, that isn't the right question. I have no way of sorting through that right now.

What happened?

I try to sift through my memory, but it's too hazy. The last thing I remember is picking up Robert's dry cleaning. The lady behind the counter wore big, turquoise earrings, and the guy behind me stood so close, I could feel his breath on my neck.

Everything after that is blank.

The two women go back and forth, Redhead searching for comfort and Combat Boots denying it.

"I wanna go home," Redhead whines before she starts to sob.

"Really? I couldn't have fucking guessed."

"Stop," I say, my voice cracking. I move my tongue around, searching for moisture, but my mouth may as well be full of cotton.

"Look at that, you woke Sleeping Beauty."

"Do you know who they are?" Redhead asks me. "What's going on?"

"I don't know." I shift, my muscles aching as I try to make my voice gentler than Combat Boots's. "But we'll figure this out together."

"Yes, together we can take over the ship. We'll use our girl power to break through metal, then—"

"Shut up," I snap. "You're not helping."

"You want helpful?" she scoffs. "I've been awake a lot longer than either of you and have had ample time to think through the rush of questions gushing through your heads right now. So let me save you some time. We're fucked. There, is that helpful?"

I ignore the snide remark and close my eyes at the sound of Redhead wailing. I don't like Combat Boots's cold pessimism, but I relate to it more than hopeless sobbing.

I'm scared. Fucking terrified. We all are. But right now, we need to use that fear to fuel us, not drain us or isolate us.

"How do you know we're on a boat?" I ask, looking around.

"Can't you feel it?"

My mind has been spinning too much to register movement, but I concentrate on it now. Sure enough, it isn't just my vision swaying. It's my whole body. The movement is slight, just a gentle up and down, but it's enough for me to pin it as the cause for my stomach flipping intermittently.

"How long do you think you've been awake?"

"It's hard to say," Combat Boots replies, the first hint of fear in her voice slipping through. She's tough, I can tell.

Good. We'll need tough.

"A couple of hours maybe," she settles on.

I nod as if that tells me anything other than wherever we're going possibly requires a long boat ride. Or they're just driving us around in circles to confuse us.

They. How do we know it's more than one man? How do we even know it's a man?

I close my eyes and run my tongue along my chapped lips, searching for some kind of relief. Or at least enough moisture to make it easier to talk.

"I'm Lib." I bump my shoulder with Red's and turn my head her way. "What's your name?"

She sniffles as she turns her head. Her green eyes meet mine, and I see so much fear in her irises it makes me want to look away, but I don't.

"Anna."

I nod then turn my head toward Combat Boots. "What about you?"

She looks at me, and I see the same fear that's in Anna's eyes but with a layer of frost over it. "Naomi."

"How about we take turns saying everything we remember. Okay?"

Naomi nods.

I take a breath and face forward to ease the strain in my neck.

It takes maybe a half hour to get through everything, but only the first minute or so of everyone's turn has to do with how we each got here. We spend the rest of the time talking about the gist of our routines, trying to figure out what we have in common.

Anna was hitchhiking when a guy in a truck picked her up and knocked her out a few miles into the drive.

Naomi was chased through a park where she sometimes crashes. She was taken by two men, one with the same description Anna gave of her guy.

And I remember absolutely nothing about my abduction.

One thing that immediately stood out to me about us is how different our situations are. Both Anna and Naomi alternate between couch hopping and being homeless. Both have no one who will report them missing. Both are prime targets for a psychopath plucking girls off the street.

I'm a Manhattan housewife. The police will start searching for me within forty-eight hours of my abduction, and my dry cleaners isn't even in a bad neighborhood. Certainly not a prime predator spot.

So ... why me?

I can tell Naomi is wondering the same, but we both keep quiet about it.

Time drags on and on, and I start to understand where her pessimism is coming from. The farther from home we get, the more hopeless our situation feels.

And then, out of nowhere, the boat stops.

Our bodies lurch, and my stomach does somersaults. Anna gasps, and for the first time since I woke up, she goes completely silent and still. We all do.

My back is to the door, so I don't see the person who swings it open. My muscles stiffen as a shuffling sounds, and I search uselessly for a weapon I know I won't find. I swallow and breathe to slow my rapid heartbeat, trying my hardest not to panic.

Wooden boards creak as two sets of footsteps travel down to us, then thump on the cabin floor.

Someone coughs. "Fuck, it smells."

Another man snickers. "Some piss themselves. You'll get used to it."

"Yeah, I don't know about that." I turn my head and barely make out a man's tattooed arms as he covers Naomi's head with a black sack. She gasps but doesn't protest. A sack is placed over my head a moment later, and Anna cries out.

"Please, let me go," she whimpers, her voice muffled by the sack. "I don't want to be here."

The cuffs clank, and a set of calloused hands touch my arm as I'm freed. My stomach revolts at the touch, but I keep quiet. I figured out it would be useless to speak to either of these men when one of them carelessly gave away that multiple women have been down here.

"Get up," one of the men growls, grabbing my shirt and yanking me up. Anna screams, and I whip my head in her direction but am shoved in another. "Walk."

I can hear Naomi and Anna shuffling behind me as I walk blindly with my hands out, guided only by the faceless man's rough touch between my shoulder blades. I bump into something solid, grateful my hands were already in front of me to catch myself on the stairs.

"Watch your step," the man says, not hiding the amusement in his voice.

I grit my teeth and carefully move up the stairs. Anna cries out again, and the apparent new guy yells at her to shut up. She screeches like she's been hit, and I stop to turn my head.

"Move." The man guiding me shoves me forward, and I expect to fall on the steps, but my palms hit a flat surface and the smell of sea salt wafts through the bag.

Warmth kisses my skin, and my blouse sticks to my back

from the humidity. Wherever we are, it's a long way from home.

I climb the rest of the way onto the deck, continuing forward when the man presses against my shoulder blade, urging me farther. My foot collides with metal, and I can see a sliver under the rim of the sack, enough for me to know I've reached the edge of the boat.

"*Go*," the guy behind me growls.

I take a big step, scared the whole time that my feet will meet nothing but water, but my foot lands on a dock.

I consider yelling out, but Anna seems to be doing enough of that for all of us, and if I'm being honest, I'm too scared. The calm I'm desperately clinging to cracks with each step I take, and my throat closes up to the point I can barely breathe.

We're pushed and prodded along a path, and I can't help but notice how unrushed the whole thing feels. They didn't bother to gag us either, which means they're confident no one will hear us. Either that or they wouldn't care.

Where the hell are we?

"Help!" Anna screams. "Somebody help me!"

"Jesus Christ, just carry the bitch," the guy at my back growls. Anna's screams intensify, then something must happen because she goes mute.

We walk for several minutes, only stopping long enough for a gate to screech open. We're guided up a set of stairs and into an air-conditioned building. Our footsteps echo off walls as we make our way to who knows where, cool, clean tile soothing my aching bare feet.

We pause while a door opens, and I'm shoved through it. A shoulder bumps mine, and the gasp that follows tells me it's Naomi.

"Finally!" a man exclaims, a friendly edge to his tone.

The black sacks are ripped off our heads, and we're met

with a tanned, smiling man rocking on his heels. His soft blond hair is combed through with natural highlights you'd imagine a surfer having, and his casual beach attire adds to the look.

"I've been anxious to meet the three of you." He looks between us with a kind smile on his face that gives the weird impression that this is all some kind of misunderstanding. I half question if I've got this wrong.

I glance at Anna and Naomi, but neither take their eyes off the smiling man.

"Welcome to Paradise Manor." He extends his hands in a welcoming gesture, and my gaze travels the room. It's a sitting room. There's just a couch, a few chairs, and a fireplace with a bookshelf on either side of it, filled with thick books having spines that don't appear to have ever been cracked.

A curtain covers the window, but it's sheer enough for me to make out green. Lots of it.

"Please, have a seat." He nods toward the couch.

"What the fuck do you want from us?" Naomi asks, her tough girl act at its finest. I mentally compliment her for it.

Anna shrinks beside her, and none of us move toward the couch.

The man's smile slowly sinks into a frown, and he sighs. He locks eyes with Naomi. "I expected nothing but directness from you, Naomi. You don't disappoint."

Naomi stiffens. "How do you know my name?"

One side of his lips twitch, like he's suppressing a smirk. "Please." He gestures toward the couch. "Sit. I'll explain everything."

Naomi and I exchange a look before trudging to the couch behind Anna. We sit, then the man pulls a chair close to us and casually plops down. I glance over at the two men who brought us here, both now guarding the door.

"Don't mind them," the tan guy says, drawing my attention back to him. He smiles warmly. "Julio and Brantley are only here to ensure that no one gets scared off."

"How do you know my name?" Naomi asks again, pointedly this time.

His eyes move back to her, and I catch the first hint of steel in them. Naomi must catch it too because the air in the room shifts and the leather couch squeaks as she sinks deeper into the cushions.

"Right, sorry. I know who you are, Naomi, because you told me. We've known each other for a while, actually. Which is how I know that under that brave exterior of yours is a scared, young woman. And I want to assure you, you're safe. So is your son, Theo."

I look at Naomi just as her eyes widen to saucers, the frost in her irises melting. Deep, suffocating, maternal dread drains her face, and I quickly look back at the man.

He turns to Anna and holds up his hand. "Before you worry, Anna, Sean is safe too. In fact, I believe he's at his first basketball game right now. If you'd like, I could have someone take a video for you. I know you've been wanting to see him play."

"What?" Anna's lip trembles. "How?"

Her face is twisted with confusion, but I see the moment something clicks into place. "Sawyer?"

He grins to confirm his identity, and it only makes me more confused.

"Pleasure to finally meet you, Anna."

"You son of a bitch," Naomi growls, jumping to her feet.

He leisurely drapes one muscular leg over the other and looks at her with a sort of amused curiosity. "Sit down, Naomi."

"Don't you fucking dare touch my son!"

"I already told you, he's safe. Safer than he was before you came here. He's being relocated to a different foster home as we speak, and this one doesn't keep locks on the fridge. He has a large trust written in his name that he'll get when he's eighteen, and no one will ever lay a finger on him again, all thanks to you. You're giving him far more by being here than you were when you were sticking needles in your arm, feeling sorry for yourself. So *sit*. Please."

"What do you want?" she rasps out, tears filling her eyes.

The man, Sawyer, sighs and stares her down until she defeatedly collapses onto the couch.

"I want the same thing you want." His voice is deceptively soothing. "I want you to be a good mother. I want you to be *clean*. And happy. And I can help with all of those things."

"I already got clean," she says, her voice holding a sad desperation.

Sawyer's face pinches skeptically. "After all the times you've thrown away your sobriety in the past, do you really think this time will stick? You need help, Naomi. There's no shame in that."

A tear slides down Naomi's cheek, and I get the urge to shake her. Five minutes with this guy, and she's already breaking down.

Who is he?

She closes her eyes.

"You told me it's what you needed, Naomi. Remember? Please let me help you."

"What about me?" Anna asks, drawing my eyes to her. She sits on the edge of the couch, leaning toward Sawyer with a glimmer of hope in her eyes I don't like.

"Yes, babygirl. I want to help you too."

"That's why we're here?" She pauses a moment, and I can see her chest inflating with her optimistic energy. "You're not going to hurt us?"

She lets out a relieved laugh, shifting to look at us like she's expecting the same reaction.

Sawyer frowns. "*Of course* not. You know I could never hurt you."

Another relieved laugh leaves her lips before her hands fly up to cover her mouth, her eyes shining with grateful tears.

Her gaze roams the room. "Is this the place you told me about?"

"Yes, it is. You'll like it, I promise." He turns back to Naomi who doesn't look at all relieved. If anything, she looks even more terrified. "And you will too, Naomi. If you decide after a few weeks that you want to go home, we can talk about it. Just give this a chance, please. Not just for me. I know you want to do the right thing for Theo too, and for now, the right thing is you being here."

She doesn't respond. She doesn't even look at him. Her eyes stare vacantly into her lap while tears drip.

"What is he talking about?" I ask, my gaze pointed at Naomi. "What is this place?"

"I don't know," she whispers, defeated.

I turn to Sawyer, but he's looking at the guards, motioning toward us with a slight nod. As I stare at him, I get a distant sense of familiarity, but I can't place him. I can't say for sure it isn't in my foggy head after hearing the other two women say they know him.

The guards come over, and Sawyer smiles at Anna. "Ladies, it has been a pleasure to meet you, and I look forward to catching up later, but for now, Julio is going to show you to your rooms."

I stand, anxious to be alone with the women again so I can ask them all of the questions making my head spin.

"Not you, Liberty," Sawyer says, gesturing for me to sit down.

The tattooed guy, Julio, takes Anna's arm and leads her away with Naomi following. I watch them go before hesitantly sitting back down.

"Cut the bullshit." I narrow my eyes at him. "It won't work on me."

He flashes me his teeth in what appears to be his first sincere expression of the day, his plastered-on kind face dissolving like sugar in boiling water. It has a sinister hue to it that matches his eyes.

I lean back into the cushions as I glance at the other man, Brantley, who's now guarding the door alone.

"I figured as much." He lets his eyes land on me, my skin crawling as he sizes me up. "I fully anticipate you being somewhat of a challenge. I prefer single moms with shit to lose, yet no one but the kiddos to miss them."

"What the *fuck* are you talking about?"

He sighs impatiently and rubs a hand over his forehead as if he's annoyed to give me any more of his time.

"All right," he says, dropping his hand. "For the sake of preserving both our time and energy, I'll keep it simple."

I sit up straight and brace for whatever he's about to tell me.

"Right now, you're on a private island thousands of miles from home. The occupants of this island pay a hefty fee to live here and carry out their lives with the utmost discretion, and with that discretion, they're allowed certain freedoms men on other shores aren't. Such as owning sex slaves."

My heart stops at his last words. My chest starts to ache, and by the time I realize I've stopped breathing, I can't even remember how my lungs work.

"I know," he says, slowly nodding as if he can read my mind. "That's a tough pill to swallow. *But* I have really good news for you, Liberty. You're one of the lucky ones. Someone has requested that you specifically remain a manor whore.

Typically, women here are sold within months, and some of the private owners have disgustingly dark tastes. If I'm being honest, some of the shit these guys are into makes me squeamish." He makes a face, but I can tell he's just poking fun at the situation. And I don't care. My pride doesn't even exist right now.

But my self-preservation does.

I dart my eyes toward the door, and before I can think of a better plan, I leap toward it. Brantley blocks the way, not looking at all concerned, and he must've expected me to back down because his eyes widen in shock when I swing my leg up and kick his bathing suit parts as hard as I can.

When he gasps and falls to the floor, I hurry around him, not looking back until I make it down the hall, relieved when I don't see Sawyer. He wasn't exaggerating when he called this place a manor... It feels like it takes forever for me to find my way out of the monstrosity.

I catch the eyes of two different men as I sprint past them. I expect to hear boots stomping after me, yells, maybe even an alarm, but only my heavy breathing fills my ears.

I know something's wrong when I make it outside and race down the path I took blind. I look over my shoulder, panic fueling me, and I cry in relief when I see no one following me. No one yells for me to stop.

I press on, and when I spot a gate, a dock, and vast ocean beyond it, I pick up my pace. My eyes dart around, and I lock eyes with a guy standing at the fence line. He covers an earpiece, his mouth moving.

Along a sidewalk on the opposite side of the gate, a man and woman walk at a brisk pace.

"Help!" I scream, pumping my legs harder. "Help me!"

The couple pauses and looks my way before I dart my eyes between them and the man with the earpiece. "Please help!"

I crash into the gate, then quickly pull myself up the metal bars and haul myself over. I drop at the feet of the couple then grab onto the man's arm. His eyes widen, and he rears back with surprise.

"I've been kidnapped," I pant out, sucking in long breaths. "Please, I'm not supposed to be here. I need to call my husband. His name is Robert Gaumond, he's the owner of Holdings Manufacturing. He…"

My eyes catch the woman's neck, and my throat closes up. I let go of the man's arm and take a step back, my eyes trailing from the loop on the black collar to the leash handle secured in the man's hand.

I lift my eyes to look at the woman's face, but she stares straight at the ground.

"You must be fresh," the man snickers, my gaze zipping back to him. Sawyer's eyes held a touch of sinisterness, but this man's eyes are all violence. All pain. All evil pleasure.

I take another step back and bump into the fence. The man laughs.

"What's your name, sweetheart?"

"She doesn't have one yet."

I jump at the sound of Sawyer's voice and spin to face him through the gate. His mouth spreads into a smile when our eyes meet.

"I'm thinking it should be something pretty, though. And full of spirit."

"Hmm," the man ponders. "Maybe a plant name."

"Clover," Sawyer suggests.

"Ivy."

"Ooh, I like that." Sawyer winks at me, then signals to the earpiece guy. The gate opens, and I'm finally zapped from my paralyzed state. I jump away from the gate, but the man easily grabs me and pins me against his chest.

"Really, Ivy?" Sawyer asks, one eyebrow raised. "You're going to run *again*? You're not a quick learner, are you?"

"Let me go!" I sneer, jerking in the man's grasp.

Sawyer steps up to me and roughly takes my chin. "Okay, Ivy. I'm going to spell this out for you one more time, so pay attention. This is a *private* island. Every person on it is fully aware of the sex slave situation. We can play the cat and mouse game if you want, but eventually, it's going to get old to me, and you're going to wind up running into someone much meaner than Mr. J. here. And while you *are* a manor whore, I'm not opposed to allowing sleepovers, so..." He lowers his eyes to my lips and loosens his grip on my chin. "Can we go back inside now so I can give you the rest of the tour? I'm sure your friends are anxious to see you."

As I stare into Sawyer's deceptively easygoing, green eyes, I feel a sense of defeat wash over me that makes every cell in my body heavier. I stand on concrete but feel as if I'm sinking into the earth.

I'm not going home. Not now, maybe not ever. If I don't find a way off this island, I'm going to live out my days as a whore, and I don't even know what all that entails.

"Why me?" I ask, my voice breaking along with my hope. It's pathetic, but part of me hopes he has soothing reassurances for me, just like he did for the other women. I wouldn't believe him, but maybe he could say something that would soften the blow. Or at least explain why and how I ended up here.

He pushes my hair back behind my ear, and I cringe.

"Why not you?" He leans in and takes a deep inhale through his nose nuzzled in my hair. "My little Manhattan peasant."

My muscles tense, and my ears heat. I can feel his lips move as he smiles.

As my heart drops into my stomach, my mind replays the

countless conversations I had with who I now know is this man. This fraud. This monster.

Saltyshells.

How could I have been so stupid?

He pulls back and grins like he's enjoying every ounce of my disgust, not only for him, but for myself. I almost agreed to meet this man. I was prepared to throw away my marriage for a shot in the dark with this piece of shit. Anger brews until my blood boils, and I channel all the hatred I have for myself into hatred for him.

I gather what little saliva I have in my mouth and spit in his face, feeling my first bout of victory when his grin falls.

4

———

LIBERTY

I slowly move my eyes toward the cellar door when it clangs open. I glare and prepare to fire venom at whoever walks through, but I won't lie and say I'm not relieved when I realize Julio isn't alone.

My glare falls and lips part as Naomi stumbles down the steps with Julio at her back. When they reach the cellar, he shoves her forward, and our eyes lock when she lifts her head. The fear that had flared in her eyes earlier has morphed into fiery hatred. Good. I'm glad I'm not the only one.

"Hurry up," Julio snaps, pushing her again. "By the other one."

She shuffles over to where I sit on the floor, and she plops down next to me without a fight. By the bruise forming on her jaw, I'd say they've beaten it out of her. For now.

I'm secured to the wall by a rusty iron clamp around my neck, and there are a whole row of similar contraptions jutting out along the wall. Julio secures Naomi's clamp, then he stands up straight and steps back.

"In case you haven't figured it out by now, fighting is

useless. Neither one of you is leaving this basement until you agree to behave."

"You say that like it's a bad thing," Naomi scoffs. "I'd rather die down here than be raped up there."

Julio chuckles, and I try not to shiver at the glint in his eyes. I keep my glare pinned on him, waiting for what I already know is about to come.

"If you say so." Julio shrugs and walks over to the water hose he tossed carelessly on the floor the last time I saw him. He swipes up the nozzle, then drags the hose to stand in front of us.

"Hold your breath," I warn Naomi, closing my eyes.

Water sprays from the hose and splatters me, but the stream isn't aimed at me this time. Naomi screams and I open my eyes and try to look her way. I can't move my head much because my skin is already rubbed raw from the restraint.

She's trying to move her head to get away from the spray, and I cringe, knowing from experience that she's tearing the skin of her neck in the process.

"Hold still," I yell over the spray. I'm rewarded with Julio sending a gust of water to my face, so I close my eyes, hold my breath, and wait for it to stop.

This goes on for another few minutes, his cruel game aimed mostly at Naomi until the water finally shuts off. He snickers as he drags the hose back where it was and tosses it down.

Icy water drips from my hair and down my body, and my shoulders convulse while I try to catch my breath. My teeth chatter, and I point my stare forward, refusing to look at Julio as he leaves. As soon as the door slams shut, I try to turn to Naomi again but give up when my neck practically screams in pain.

I reach out to her instead, my hand finding hers and squeezing while I wait for her sobs to cease.

"Fuck those guys," she says, her voice cracking.

I move my eyes to the door. "Especially Julio."

Naomi huffs. "Julio is just a tool. *Sawyer* did this."

Sawyer's image enters my mind again, and anger tears through my core. After I spit in his face, he wasn't so calm anymore. He dragged me back to the manor by my hair, then had Julio bring me to the cellar. I haven't seen him since.

I clamp my teeth down to stop the shaking, and after a minute, I speak again. "You met him on a chat site, didn't you?"

Naomi sighs. "Yes. I'm guessing you did too?"

"He never told me his name, but yeah, I did. He pretended to be some lonely guy acting as a caretaker for his paralyzed wife."

Naomi laughs dryly. "He put more effort into lying to you."

"What makes you say that?"

Her legs move as she shifts to find a more comfortable position. She's going to be disappointed. I've been searching for some sort of comfort since I got here. There isn't any.

"It took him a little while to tell me his name, but he actually did mention the island. Obviously, not everything that it entailed, but he had said he lived on one and that the people here were into kink. He offered to pay me to come here, and I nearly did, but I told him I couldn't leave my son. The site I met him on… It was um… It was through an ad I put up during a really shitty time in my life. I'd just lost custody of my son, and I was desperate for money. It's the same story with Anna. He told her he wanted her here so he could spoil her *Pretty Woman* style, that he loved her, and a whole bunch of other bullshit that he's still somehow getting her to believe. Most of the rest of them are just as delusional."

"The rest of them?" I ask, my stomach turning.

"Yeah. There's like ten other women up there who share the same quarters. Some of them came to the island willingly because they thought they were coming here to be with Sawyer. Two were taken and brought here a couple of weeks ago, and they're way more wary than the rest, but even they are acting like they've just accepted this."

"What is 'this' exactly? He told me I was going to be a manor whore. What does that mean?"

"It means you're supposed to fuck the guys who come here until you're fully brainwashed, and then I think you get sold to one person and go live with them. I'm really not sure, though. The woman I talked to seemed *excited* to be picked by a 'master' who's coming to get her soon. That's the gist of what I picked up on. Like I said on the boat, we're fucked."

"No, we're not." I swallow, trying to convince myself I'm not lying. "There has to be a way off this island."

"There isn't. Trust me."

"You've only been here a few hours, Naomi. You can't possibly know that."

There's a pause, and tension fills the cellar like a heavy fog. I shift, the discomfort in my mind worse than anything physical at this point. My limbs went numb to the concrete floor a long time ago.

"How long do you think we've been here?" Naomi asks, the concern in her voice putting me even more on edge.

"I don't know. A while." I try to count the number of times I've dozed off out of boredom or exhaustion, but I can't remember.

"Lib… We got here three days ago."

5

ANGEL

"**F**ucking lost cause."

Sawyer shakes his head disapprovingly while he stares at the monitor showing surveillance footage of the cellar. Lib sits in the lone cell with her knees pulled up to her chest and her arms snugly wrapped around her shins like she's holding herself in. Sawyer says she's been like that for three days.

I'll admit, I expected much better progress than this. I've been gone a week, and that's typically enough time for Sawyer to have a woman coaxed into submission. The cellar is a last resort sort of thing, so Lib must be fighting hard. I'm as impressed as I am annoyed.

My eyes travel to the wall of empty neck binds, and I consider asking why she isn't in one of them but stop myself. It's telling that she's in the cell. Sawyer never uses it. It's for long term misbehavior, meant to punish while limiting the muscle atrophy that would occur from being in one position for too long. In a way, the cell is an admission of failure.

"There's no such thing as a lost cause." My eyes travel back to Lib. She hasn't flinched.

Sawyer scoffs. "Right."

"She just needs more time." I tilt my head as I study her. I'm not even convincing myself.

Sawyer shakes his head. "I should've never accepted her from Gaumond. She's not the type of woman who fits in here."

"You wanted a challenge."

Sawyer clenches his jaw and stares at Lib's image with more disdain than I think is necessary. She's really gotten to him.

"Yes, well, I was wrong," he grumbles, craning his neck. "I'm giving her two more days, then she's gone."

"Gone, as in…?"

He doesn't answer, but he doesn't have to. No slave leaves the island. Ever. Under any circumstances. Any woman brought here dies here, whether they outlive their time as a whore or not. Older women take over the more domestic tasks once they're no longer wanted sexually. It's against the law of the island to murder a slave, but there are always exceptions.

"That bad, huh?" I ask.

He turns to me and holds up his hand, showing me broken skin with teeth indentations just below his knuckles.

I fight a smile.

"We stopped giving her food three days ago. If starvation isn't enough to make her behave, I don't know what is. I'm not a fan of torture, but Julio hasn't exactly been gentle, so I doubt even that would work. The next time Gaumond shows up here, I'm kicking his ass. The asshole said she was a passive housewife. The bitch is feral."

I chuckle and earn Sawyer's glare.

"I'm glad you find this amusing."

"Are you sure she doesn't recognize you? Maybe she's pissed that her husband pimped her out."

He shakes his head. "She doesn't know about that."

"How can you be so sure?"

"Because the second she had a chance, she ran screaming for help and asked Joseph Castor to call her husband. I'm pretty sure if she recognized me, she would've mentioned it. I met her briefly once, what, four years ago?"

"Five," I correct. "It was when we first started business with Gaumond."

Sawyer waves this off like it doesn't make a difference, which is true. "The point is, she's not acclimating, and I'm done wasting my energy on her. If you want her, take her. But I don't want her at the manor anymore."

I look at the screen again and consider it for a second before dismissing the idea. "You know it's against the rules for me to have my own slave."

"Yeah, well, los que hacen las algunos, or whatever the hell you say."

"It's *los que hacen las reglas hacen las lagunas*, but close." *Those who make the rules, make the loopholes.*

One side of my lips lift in an amused smile that Sawyer doesn't return.

"Give me a chance with her," I say, going back to the screen. "Maybe she needs a gentler touch."

His eyes narrow. "You never want anything to do with the new whores."

I shrug. "I like a challenge too."

"I'm the king of 'good cop, bad cop,' Angel. It's not going to work."

"Maybe because you play it with your two personalities."

He sways his head like he's considering my words, then nods. "Okay, that's probably fair. But it still won't work on this girl."

I give one last look at the screen before backpedaling a few steps and glancing at Sawyer. "We'll see."

As I leave Sawyer's office, he throws a sarcastic "good luck" at my back. I stop in the kitchen and grab a granola bar to tuck into my slacks' pocket. I just got back to the island an hour ago and haven't changed out of my suit. I prefer it that way, though. Sawyer is the one who's into the relaxed, beach-life look.

As humorous as I find his inability to tame Lib, I'm annoyed with him. I fully anticipated her being acclimated once I got back, and I've been looking forward to it all week. Actually, I've been looking forward to it for five years.

I suppose I can be patient a little longer.

I get to the cellar door and roll my neck, forcing out all expectations of what's about to go down.

She could recognize me. That thought has occurred to me before, but I didn't think much of it then. She was supposed to be an obedient whore the first time I saw her here, so what the hell would it matter if she recognized me? But now it does. It could make things worse. Or it could make things better. I'm not sure.

It might not matter. Like Sawyer said, it's been five years. It's highly possible I didn't make the same lasting impression on her that she made on me.

Only one way to find out.

I unlatch the cellar door and gently pull it open before making my way down the wooden stairs. When I step onto concrete, I look into the cell and find Lib's eyes. She stares me down like she's sizing me up for a fight as I slowly walk to stand in front of the cell. My lips are drawn into a frown although inside I'm smiling.

Five years, and I'm finally standing in front of Lib, with her at my complete mercy. A shiver travels down my spine, but I don't let any of the excitement show on my face.

She's caked in dust and grime right now, but she's still the most stunning woman I've ever seen. I could kiss her right now... Fuck her right here on the concrete and it would be just as good as any bed.

That's not an option yet.

I force my thoughts to center and stare at her as if she's any other girl. "Hello," I say, ensuring that the disapproving frown on my face remains.

"What the fuck do you want?" she snaps, her eyes narrowed to slits.

I try to gauge whether she recognizes me, but I can't tell. From what I've heard, she aims her hatred at anyone who steps foot down here, so this may be her norm.

I pull the granola bar from my pocket and hold it up for her to see. Her eyes widen a moment, but she quickly recovers and goes back to glaring.

"I thought you might be hungry."

"Go fuck yourself."

I lower the granola bar and glance at the jugs of water sitting in the corner next to her. "I'm told your name is Ivy." I move my eyes back to her. "Is that true?"

No response.

"I'm going to take that as a yes. I understand you want to keep your pride, Ivy. I get it. You've been stripped of your freedom, and you feel like playing nice would be giving in, and maybe you're right. So I won't ask you to. You don't owe me anything." I bend and extend my arm through the bars, placing the meager offering on the floor before I stand back up, turn, and force myself to walk away.

"Wait," she says when I'm halfway up the steps. Her voice is barely loud enough for me to hear, and I question if I heard it at all. I look over my shoulder and see she hasn't moved from her seated position. The granola bar is where I left it.

We lock eyes, and in hers I see so much despair that the frown my lips pull into is genuine this time. I turn fully but don't descend the steps.

"Yes?" I call out.

"Is Naomi okay?"

"Naomi?" I ask although I know exactly who she's referring to. Her new name is April, and she's one of the women who came here with Lib. Apparently, she put up a decent fight the first few days, but she's back upstairs and cooperating.

"April," Lib corrects. She clears her throat. "Is April okay?"

I slowly walk back down and over to the cell. I lean against the bars and peer inside. "Is she your friend?"

No response. No surprise.

"I don't know an April." It's a half truth. I've never met her. "But I could find out who she is and if she's okay. If it's important to you."

Lib's eyes bounce around my face as she studies me, her brows slightly pinched. I wonder what she sees. Just another monster, I'm sure.

"Who are you?" she asks. She narrows her eyes skeptically, like she's bracing herself for a lie or for a truth she doesn't want to hear.

I take a moment to think through what I want to say. She's given me practically nothing, so I'd like to leave her curious.

"Mr. A," I settle on. "I'm a resident of the island."

There's a pause while she digests that, her pretty eyes searching me for more information. "Why are you down here?"

I give a small shrug like even I don't know the answer to that. "I heard you were having a hard time."

Before she has a chance to ask another question, I turn on my heel and walk away. She doesn't ask me to wait this time, and when I make it out of the cellar, I find Sawyer waiting for me with a smirk on his face.

"Better luck next time, bud." He claps me on the shoulder

and turns to wrap the chain around the door handle. He looks over his shoulder before speaking again. "I have to hand it to you though… The fact that she didn't try to attack you is impressive."

"She needs patience. Be gentle and she'll quit biting."

He laughs. "If you say so."

He fumbles with the padlock, still snickering as if this is amusing. As if this isn't a woman's life we're talking about.

"Give it time," I say, my tone serious enough to snuff out his humor. "She'll come around."

He clicks the lock into place then turns to me. "You think so?"

I nod and pat his shoulder before walking past him. "I'll be back tomorrow."

6

LIBERTY

I hold my breath when I hear the cellar door open.

Mr. A walks in, and I let it out, my shoulders sagging with a relief I'm disappointed in myself for having.

I don't *want* to want him here. I want to dread his presence just like I do every other man I've seen since I was abducted. But he's given me something I've been missing since I got here, and it's somehow breaking me down more than anything else these sick fucks have tried.

Because of Mr. A, I finally have a better sense of time.

He comes once a day, gently places a granola bar into the cell, then leaves without ever saying a word. He's done this four times, always wearing different clothes, so I'm almost certain that when Mr. A comes, it's a new day. It even feels like I'm beginning to get a sense for when he's about to arrive, so I think he even shows up at the same time. But that could be in my head.

There are no windows in this cellar, and having no obvious patterns, I can't get a sense of Julio's schedule. He shows up to fuck with me and to dump the toilet—which is just a plastic bucket…gross, I know—but there's no internal clock clueing me in to how often that is. My stomach cramps worsen as time passes, to the point I spend a good chunk of the day—or night?—lying on my side, curled into a ball, wishing the pain would ease, but that's the only indication that I've been here for a substantial amount of time.

Until now. Now I can tell how much time passes, and it makes things worse while simultaneously bringing comfort. I have something to wait for, something to crave, something to look forward to. That fucking daily granola bar.

Sharp pain seizes my stomach, and I wrap my arms around myself and squeeze, waiting for it to pass. Normally, I fight through it when someone else is here—I don't like to show my pain—but today, I don't care. Julio already came. I've already used my energy putting on a show for him. I don't have any left.

At least that's what I tell myself.

I open my eyes as Mr. A walks up and crouches to place the bar in the cell. I stare at his tan face and can't help but notice how handsome he is. Today especially. He's wearing black slacks and a white button-down he has rolled up his forearms. The top two buttons are undone, and he's missing a tie today. His chestnut brown hair is tousled like he's been running his hands through it, and his hard jawline sprouts stubble I haven't seen before.

I wonder what his days look like. What made him run his hand through his hair? Where has he been? What has he been doing?

This is an island meant for play, but he looks like he does nothing but work. He doesn't have the same casual attire as the others, and he always looks serious. There's no evil in his eyes, and he isn't annoyingly carefree like Sawyer. I haven't caught a single smirk to tell me he gets pleasure from seeing me in pain, unlike the others. He doesn't try to take anything from me or convince me that everything's going to be okay, and all of this combined makes me hate him just a little bit less than Sawyer and Julio.

Who is he? I spend just about every moment I'm not plotting my escape imagining his life, coming up with characters who may resemble him. Some of them are vile, cruel, ruthless. Sometimes I let myself imagine he's kind, as if anyone on this island is capable of that. I don't know his motive for coming down here, but it's hard not to sometimes imagine that maybe he just gives a shit.

I've been determined not to show my weakness, not to give these people any of the begging I know they're after, but I'm breaking. I can feel it. I'm stripped down to my bra and panties, and my knees feel rough against my arms. My skin is dirty and dry. My stomach gnaws like I'm being eaten from the inside. I'm exhausted all the time. And I'm so lonely. If I'm going to break, I don't want the other two to be the ones who watch it happen. If any of these assholes is going to see me vulnerable ... I guess I'd want it to be him.

I try to meet his eyes, waiting for the moment he looks at me. I want him to see what's in my head, see how badly I'm hurting, how terrified I am, and how fucking miserable it is constantly hiding these things. I want him to talk to me again. To say hello. Say goodbye. Say anything.

I will him to look at me, but it doesn't work. He stands up straight, turns around, then walks back toward the stairs.

My eyes water as I move my gaze to the granola bar. A piercing pain lights up my stomach, and I suck in a sharp breath, air whistling past my teeth. I close my eyes and swallow.

"Thank you," I call out, moisture coating my lashes.

His footsteps stop echoing on the walls, and even though my eyes are closed, I can feel his stare. Or maybe I'm just hoping for it. Maybe he's already left.

I open my eyes at that thought and lift my head to see him

paused on the bottom step. His back is to me, and he doesn't turn around. After a moment, he continues up the stairs. I bite down on my lip.

Don't go.

Don't go.

"Don't go," I blurt out, tucking my face into my knees and letting my tears slicken my skin.

I don't look up, but I hear his footsteps coming toward me. When they stop, I lift my head, wipe my eyes, and force myself to calm. I won't beg. I promised myself I wouldn't do that.

"Are you okay, Ivy?"

My vision blurs, and I don't answer. That question doesn't deserve a response.

"Would you like to talk?" he asks, his voice light. Gentle.

Fuck, I hate him. I don't know him, but I hate him. He's like a lifeboat in the distance, leisurely drifting this way, but I'm already drowning, and he must know it.

How pathetic do I look right now?

Anger heats my skin, melding with so much grief that it's a confusing combination.

Don't go.

I hate you.

Help me.

Kill yourself.

Confusing. Just so fucking confusing.

"Okay," he says, turning his back to me.

"Why are you here?" my voice cracks.

He sighs and turns to face me. His palm extends, gesturing toward the meager offering. "I thought you might be hungry."

"I'm not stupid." I take a breath and try to make my voice steady. "I know this is some kind of fucked-up game you're playing with me. If you felt bad for me, you'd bring more than a granola bar."

He frowns then glances down at the offering like he's just now considering that. If he's acting, he's doing a good job.

Sawyer was able to subdue the other women. He was able to confuse them, just like I'm confused now. Is that what this guy's trying to do to me? Subdue me, tame me, trick me like they've tricked the others?

Who *is* he?

And if he is just trying to pacify me … why is it working so well?

"Would you like something else to eat?" he asks, his voice deceptively innocent. "We could go upstairs. I think there's plenty of dinner left over. Margarette made roasted duck."

My stomach twists, and I try not to let the pain show on my face. He gave me another piece of information with that, although I'm not sure it was worth the imagery that makes my mouth water.

It's nighttime.

"And what would we do after?" I ask, injecting venom into my words. "I'm assuming you'd expect me to sleep with you."

He raises a brow like I'm being crazy. Like I'm not a prisoner on an island of sex slaves.

"I want to phrase this as delicately as I can because I'd hate for you to take offense, but you aren't exactly in the best shape to be lustworthy. I think you could use a few good meals and at least one good night's sleep. A shower wouldn't hurt."

"So that I can make myself 'lustworthy?' "

"No, so that you don't die."

My lungs seize at that. I know it's stupid because, of course, they'll eventually kill me. It's been a struggle determining which fate is worse, dying or giving in. I still don't know, but hearing the possibility of them killing me out loud makes it scarier somehow.

"The human body can survive about two months without food, as long as it's hydrated. That's *without* the little bit of food I'm bringing you. You have plenty of time to continue your hunger strike if that's what you want, but I'd suggest ending it sooner rather than later. You're getting dangerously close to mental health damage you won't be able to come back from. Sawyer is forgiving, but he has his limits, and a slave who starts rubbing feces on the walls is one of them. You understand what I'm saying?"

I look down at my knees as my mind goes to the food mere feet away. I could devour it in a single bite. I just don't want to do it in front of Mr. A.

"I'm not on a hunger strike. I'm being starved."

"You're being *stubborn*," Mr. A counters. He lifts his eyes and points to the camera overlooking the cell. "You have the option of going upstairs with the rest of the whores anytime you choose. Just say the word."

"Don't call us that," I snarl, my eyes narrowing.

Mr. A sighs like my dignity is a nuisance. "Staying down here is a choice, Ivy. It's not one anyone wants you to make. Pitying yourself isn't doing you any good, and neither is being prideful."

"If I go up there..." I inhale a shaky breath. "We both know what happens."

"I know what happens. You seem a bit hazy about it."

"Naomi told me. You force women to have sex with residents like you, and then you sell them to the first person who's interested. Sawyer even told me that, so stop trying to bullshit me."

Mr. A stares at me without saying anything. For a moment, it's a welcome stare down, but then my skin begins to crawl.

"I'm going to ask you a question that you aren't going to like. But I want you to put that fighting spirit of yours aside when I'm gone and truly think about it. Okay?"

I press my lips together and remain still.

"You're on an island with more wealth than you could know what to do with. You live in a mansion beside the ocean. You'll eat great food, wear designer clothes, pursue as many hobbies as you want, and never have to worry about anything for the rest of your life. Someone will always take care of your every need, forever. And yes, in return, you're expected to meet the physical needs of those who take care of you. You're expected to be obedient."

"Is your question coming anytime soon?"

His face sobers, and there's no trace of empathy left in his expression. I was right... He doesn't feel bad for me. He's as vile as all the other men here, malevolent eyes or not. What did I expect him to do? *Save* me? *Understand*? Why? Because he brings me fucking *crumbs*?

My face heats with fresh anger, and it's good because it distracts me from my sinking heart.

"How different do you think this is from the life you'd chosen for yourself?"

My jaw goes slack, and my chest aches. I'm stunned. Not because he knows more about me than I'd realized. Not because I can't believe he'd have the audacity to ask me that.

I'm stunned because instantly, I know what he means. And finally, I know why they picked me to come here.

Because they think I'm a gold digger. And they see this as a gold digger's paradise. I told saltyshells—Sawyer— everything, *everything* that Robert put me through. So not only am I a gold digger in their eyes, but I'm also a doormat.

They probably had no idea I'd fight back.

"I won't be back," Mr. A says, his face hard. He turns and

takes a few steps before looking over his shoulder. "I hope to see you around, Ivy."

With that, he's gone. And for the first time, I don't hide my tears. They flow down my face freely, and a sob barrels up my chest.

Finally, I break.

7

———

ANGEL

$\mathcal{M}$y eyes roam the playroom, the low lighting making it hard to recognize faces. Light flickers like this is a nightclub—Sawyer's taste, not mine—and I catch glimpses of women, but none resemble the blue-eyed beauty I'm searching for.

Yesterday, Sawyer told me she was being moved upstairs. I can't remember a time when I've felt more relieved. I've been wanting Lib for years, and her stubbornness was beginning to make me think I'd never get my chance. Acting as if I'd given up on her was risky, but it was only hours before Sawyer called and told me she'd caved.

That gave her twenty-four hours to get cleaned up and rested for tonight. I didn't ask Sawyer if she'd be here because I didn't want to seem too eager, but now I regret that. If she doesn't show up, I'll have endured Sawyer's affinity for strobe lights and club music for no reason.

I'd been lingering at a table off to the side of the playroom, but now I make my way to the bar on the other side. To call this a 'room' is a bit misleading considering the square footage of this space must be more than most houses.

Tables for two line a portion of both walls with two fully stocked bars on opposite sides of the room.

Several stages with poles and cages occupy the middle of the space with plenty of chairs surrounding them.

Couches are strategically placed on both ends, and various equipment is sprinkled throughout. Sibians, spanking horses, and pillories … one of which is currently being used to lock a girl in place while several men line up behind her. I watch her face twist with ecstasy and think I hear her moan, but it's too loud in here to be sure.

The music blares, and the sounds of people fucking mix into a cocktail that can make any man hard. If I wasn't slyly searching for Lib, I'd already be partaking.

In the back of my mind, I consider the possibility that Lib is already engaging in the fun. Jealousy sits like a weight in my mind, but I don't allow it to claw its way to the forefront. Lib isn't mine to have, she's mine to share. That'll have to be good enough.

Amari, a regular bartender, is working tonight. She bustles around, hurrying to make drinks for the six or so people waiting. She meets my eyes and winks.

"Hey, gorgeous," I mouth, a smile plastered on my face. Shiny sequins dot beneath her eyes, and her makeup is laid on so thick, it'd be hard to recognize her if she wasn't working the bar. She's been here for nearly a decade and is in her early forties, but I personally don't understand why Sawyer doesn't have her joining in on the fun anymore. She's one of my favorite women here.

She holds up a finger and finishes making a drink for someone.

"How are you, tonight?" she asks once she's done, pulling out a glass and setting it in front of me. She grabs a bottle of whiskey and pours while keeping her eyes on me. She has this shit down to a science.

"I'm doing well. Would be better if you weren't working."

She chuckles and rolls her eyes before her gaze flicks to a guy who steps up beside me and leans across the bar to request a shot of tequila. Even in the heavily-scented room, I can smell the alcohol wafting off of him. She takes his order and swiftly grabs another glass.

"Right," she says to me, unconvinced.

I pick up my glass and take a drink of the amber liquor, savoring the way it burns on the way down. "Been a while, huh?"

"Too long." She finishes up the guy's drink, then slides it to him, displaying what is obviously a forced smile when he says something I don't make out over the music. Her smile falls as soon as he walks away, then she turns back to me while grabbing more glasses from under the bar. "Desiree was looking for you earlier."

My jaw tics. "Oh, yeah?" I look over my shoulder as if Desiree will be standing behind me.

"Said you haven't come to see her lately."

"I've been busy."

She narrows her eyes skeptically, a smirk playing on her lips. "You're always busy. That's a terrible excuse."

"I'll think of something better."

She looks behind me and dips her chin. "You'd better think fast."

Before I can turn, a hand wraps around my arm and another covers my eyes. Desiree's perfume stands out among the cloud of sweat and sex, and her lip gloss sticks to my ear when she presses her mouth against it. "Guess who?"

Shit.

She removes her hand, and I down the rest of the whiskey before turning to her and forcing a smile. "Hey."

"Hey yourself." She winks and lifts onto her toes to kiss me.

I let her lips linger on mine for a moment before gently pulling away. I wipe away her cherry lip gloss with the back of my hand and clear my throat.

"Where have you been?" she asks, her lips softening into a pout I found cute two weeks ago but now has me annoyed. "I've missed you."

"I know, I've missed you too. Work has been crazy lately."

"Aww, poor guy." She pouts again and runs her hands down my chest while I try not to recoil. "Lucky for you, I know a great stress reliever."

She lowers her hands to my belt and tugs while sliding her tongue over her bottom lip.

I look over her shoulder, searching for Lib yet again, and when I don't see her, I almost consider taking Desiree up on her offer. I'm hard, and I'm beginning to get impatient. But I know anything short of Lib would be a letdown.

"That sounds nice." I move my eyes back to Desiree. "I wish I could, but I'm actually looking for someone. There's a new girl who's been having a hard time, and Sawyer asked me to check in on her. Make sure she's acclimating well. Her name's Ivy. Do you happen to know where she is?"

Desiree arches a brow. "Sawyer asked you to check in on her?"

I nod.

"That girl isn't working tonight. I'm pretty sure she's in trouble."

My eyes narrow. "What do you mean?"

Desiree shrugs. "I heard she hit Julio over the head with a lamp. I don't know for sure because Sawyer isn't letting her stay with the rest of us, but that's the rumor. Julio has a bandage over his ear today, though, so I think there's some truth to it."

You have to be fucking kidding me.

I clench my jaw and subtly shrug away from Desiree's hands.

"Why would Sawyer ask you to check in on her?" Desiree asks, a confused crinkle between her eyes. It never occurred to me until now how annoyingly clueless she is. All smiles, all the time. Eager to please. A jealous nature I used to find attractive. And dumb. Really fucking dumb.

"I don't know. Did he put her back in the cellar?"

"Honestly, I'm not sure she's even here anymore... You know what I mean?"

My skin heats, and the noise in the playroom is suddenly deafening. I nod at Desiree, then lean in to speak in her ear. "I have to go. I'll see you later."

She grabs my arm and calls for me to wait, but I yank out of her hold and make my way toward the door. My jaw is tight as I weave around people, and when someone bumps into me, my hands ball into fists. I get the urge to swing at someone, anyone at this point, but I let it go and stomp out of the playroom.

I make a beeline for Sawyer's office, and in the minute it takes to get there, my anger has boiled over. My hand is on the doorknob when I consider changing my destination and seeking out Julio instead, but I close my eyes, take a steadying breath, then try to twist the knob. It's locked.

"You all right, man?"

It's Sawyer's voice.

I open my eyes and turn my head to my right where he stands a few feet away, scratching at his cheek.

"Where is she?" I ask, my voice harder than it should be. I need to reign it in. I know that, and yet it's taking all I have not to punch the innocent expression off Sawyer's face.

"Where's who?"

"Lib."

He tilts his head, my question still not registering.

"Ivy. Where's Ivy?"

Recognition flares, and he straightens. "Oh, her. She's in one of the bedrooms. Bitch is still being a pain in the ass, but you were right, she's getting there. I'm keeping her from the other girls so she doesn't try to start a revolution." He laughs. "That's why she's not in the playroom, if you were looking for her there. I don't think she's ready for it. In fact, I'd bet a thousand someone would be getting their dick bit tonight… So, you're welcome."

"Why didn't you tell me any of this?"

Sawyer squints at me. "Seriously?"

"I've been standing around for an hour looking for her. Your strobe lights about made me have a seizure."

He chuckles then lets his lips relax into a wicked, lopsided grin. "Jesus, dude. This woman has you on edge, and she isn't even your problem. *Relax*. Go pick one of the rooms upstairs, and I'll send one of the girls up to help you get rid of some of that frustration. It's not happenin' with what's-her-face tonight."

I pull in a deep breath and flex my fingers at my sides, letting blood flow into them. My muscles slowly loosen, and I roll my neck.

"Are you okay?"

I blink and look at Sawyer. "Yeah, sorry," I say, finally coming to my senses. "Fucking Desiree made it sound like you'd killed Ivy or something and didn't bother to tell me."

"Is that the rumor?" Sawyer leans one shoulder against the wall and tucks his hands into his pockets.

"It was a guess."

"And if it were true… Would it really matter that much to you? You don't even know her, Angel. Why are you so hung up on this chick?"

I consider his question even though I have no intention of answering. I understand his confusion. I've spent a chunk of my life on this island, yet never once gotten this invested in a manor whore. I haven't had a girlfriend since college, and honestly, the idea of being monogamous leaves me feeling suffocated. So why does this woman have such a hold on me?

It's simple... I can't have her.

I wanted her years ago, and I let myself walk away, thinking she'd be a distant memory before I ever left New York City. But that didn't happen. I thought about her, occasionally checked up on her, patiently waiting for her to come to her senses about Robert Gaumond. I was merely curious, but when I fed that curiosity, time and time again it turned into something bigger. Something, dare I say, obsessive.

She didn't leave Gaumond. She married him. And that made it so much worse because underneath my success, my calm, my patience, I'm a child who can't stand the idea of not getting something I want.

So to finally get the opportunity, to finally get the chance to scratch this itch just to have it swept away in one careless move, would drive me mad. It'd forever be there, like the shiny toy in a claw machine when I've run out of quarters.

"Which room is she in?" I ask.

Sawyer sighs, pressing his tongue into his cheek. He takes his time answering. "On this floor. Cooper is standing guard."

I give a curt nod and start down the hallway.

"Careful, friend. She's armed and dangerous."

I wave a hand over my shoulder and continue without looking back.

I find Cooper standing in front of a bedroom door, and I don't bother to address him when I approach. He must sense my conviction because he steps to the side and looks straight ahead like he doesn't see me.

I fling open the door and step into the room.

8

ANGEL

$\mathcal{M}$y eyes lock with Lib's, and I watch her posture change as soon as she registers it's me.

The taut muscles of her shoulders relax, and her face softens from fearful to relieved. For a moment, that trips me up. I have to remind myself it's what I want and what I was trying to achieve.

It isn't bad, just … different. I've grown close-ish with a few women in the manor, but when they first arrived, it took each one of them a while to relax around me. They hear too many rumors.

"What do you want?" she asks, her eyes darkening like she just remembered she's supposed to keep her walls up.

Her hands are tucked underneath the comforter, and I move my eyes between them and the headboard. It's one of those with small wooden rods lined up across the back, and one of the rods is missing. Wood is splintered at the top of the headboard where the rods attach.

She couldn't possibly be more obvious.

I sigh and walk up to the bed, holding out my hand.

She glares at me and shifts with her hands still beneath the comforter.

"Give it to me, Ivy."

Her teeth are clenched, and her long, wavy hair frames her guarded face in a way that makes her look more cute than fierce. The pink cami top with white lace at the seams doesn't help her warrior act either.

We stare at each other, neither of us blinking until she finally looks away. She slowly pulls the wooden rod, split at the tip to form a jagged edge, from beneath the covers, and she hands it to me.

I toss it across the room, then turn back to her and shake my head. "You have to stop doing this shit."

"I will. Just as soon as you let me go."

I open my mouth to respond but end up closing it and pinching the bridge of my nose. She knows she isn't going to be let go. There's no point in saying it.

A frustrated breath rushes past my lips as I sit on the side of the bed. I roll my shoulders and take deep, slow inhales, trying to ease my annoyance.

A wooden rod? Really? That's what she thinks could take me down?

"I thought you said you wouldn't be back." I assume she means for her tone to be condescending, but I catch the hope in it. She's glad I'm here. Why, I'm not sure. As far as I'm aware, she's no longer being starved.

Does she want something else?

I turn my head to face her. "Should I leave?"

Her lips form a straight line, and she stares at me without saying anything.

"Yes? No?"

"I think you people have made it clear that I don't have a choice in the matter."

"Sure you do. I'm giving you one right now."

She remains quiet, and I spend the silence trying to read her face. She looks conflicted. Her lips in a tight line say one thing, but her imploring eyes say another.

I stand from the bed and take a step toward the door, feeling her eyes on my back. A desperate kind of tension clouds the room.

"What kind of influence do you have on Sawyer?" she asks, stopping me. I consider ignoring the question and leaving, just to discourage her from playing this game. She's silent, I walk away, she speaks. How many times are we going to do this?

I turn and slide my hands into my pockets, donning a mask of indifference to cover up my irritation. "Some. Why?"

She bites her lip and takes her time answering.

"Ivy?"

"Hmm?"

"Would you like my help with something?"

She takes a few deep breaths, then nods.

I walk back to the bed and sit.

"I don't want Julio to come near me." Her eyes flicker with fear, and she shifts the blanket like the temperature in the room dropped.

"Are you afraid he's angry with you?" I ask, injecting sympathy into my words. I figure it's best to soften the defensiveness I know she's about to feel. "If you had hit me over the head with a lamp, I'd be angry with you too. I know you're scared, but these decisions you're making don't come without consequences."

"It wasn't a lamp." She gives her head a shake and lowers her eyes. "It was a water glass. And I had a good reason this time."

I try not to roll my eyes with skepticism. "And what would that be?"

"He was going to rape me." Her voice shakes, and she

keeps her gaze aimed at the bed. Genuine fear—which I've only seen in spurts—floods her face like she just took a mask off to reveal it.

My muscles bunch, and anger snakes its way inside of me, taking hold just as it did a half hour ago.

"You asked me what the difference is between being here and the life I had before, and for a while, I thought maybe you had a point. But my husband never held me down to rape me. He never locked me in a cellar or room and starved me. You people think—"

"Julio held you down?" I ask, my jaw clenching.

Lib finally looks at me, studies my face for a moment, then nods.

That son of a bitch.

A fire rages inside of me, and every muscle I have itches to propel me from this room, find Julio, and strangle him.

But I don't move. I continue sitting on the bed with Lib and try not to let my head explode.

"He shouldn't have done that." I take a steadying breath. "That's not the kind of thing we condone here."

"Are you fucking with me?" she scoffs. "Sawyer told me the day I got here that some of the men on this island have 'disgustingly dark tastes.' Why are you so hellbent on selling this life to me? Even if I was an idiot and believed the bullshit you say, do you think I wouldn't find out the truth eventually? Please, just—"

"You're right," I cut her off before she can continue her tirade. "Individual owners don't have a lot of rules. There are *some*, but not many. But here, in the manor, Sawyer makes the rules. And I know for a fact that rape is not allowed. You're a manor whore, and you're expected to act like one, but no one should be physically forcing you. That's the reason you're here right now instead of on your back with someone else."

"Sawyer doesn't believe me," she says, turning so she's fully facing me. "He thinks I just said Julio did that so he wouldn't throw me back in the basement. Even if he did believe me, he acted like it wouldn't be a big deal if it were true. And he didn't say he'd ban Julio from coming in here."

Her eyes are wide and hopeful, and as much as I don't want to believe her, she isn't a good enough actress to pull off this façade.

What the fuck, Sawyer?

"I'll take care of it," I say, keeping my voice level. I swallow my anger, doing my best to set it aside for later. "Is there anything else you need?"

She stares at me for a moment, her brow slightly pinched like she's unsure of something. "How are you going to take care of it?"

"I'm going to kill him."

"What?" Her eyes go wide with surprise.

Now it's my brow's turn to pinch. "You said he held you down with the intention of raping you."

"Right, but. I just…" Her mouth hangs open, and her eyes flicker around while she tries to form words.

"Do you not want him dead?" I ask, even more confused.

"No, I… I don't know." She blinks and looks off like she's considering something. "Are you serious right now?"

Why would I be joking?

I keep my mouth shut while she stares at me in disbelief.

"You would… You'd…"

"I'd what?" I look at her expectantly, but I'm now beginning to pick up what's going on in her head. This is yet another first for me. Most of the manor whores hear the rumors about me long before I meet them. Lib hasn't, which means she has no idea I'm capable of killing someone … yet. She'll find out soon enough.

She swallows forcefully enough that I hear it, and she closes her eyes. "You're a murderer?"

I nearly laugh at the astonished way she says it.

"I'm not a fan of labels, so I'm going to ignore that question."

She looks down at the comforter and picks at a loose strand in the seam. "What if I'd been lying?"

"Were you?"

"No."

"Then we don't need to 'what if.'"

Her eyes raise to look at me. "Why would you believe me over one of your own people?"

I shake my head. "He isn't one of 'my people.' I don't work here, I just live on the island, and I'm friends with Sawyer. Julio means nothing to me."

"Okay," she drags out the word, eyeing me skeptically. "You keep saying I'm a manor whore. Why would *I* mean something to you?"

I open my mouth, then close it once I realize she has a point. I'm not supposed to know Lib. I don't know Julio either, but I know that the kind of men Sawyer hires aren't the kind the world needs.

But to *kill* him for this? For a woman I've supposedly just met? A disobedient one at that. And with no proof.

It does sound drastic.

But I don't really care. I'm not going to be able to sleep knowing what the piece of shit could possibly do to Lib. Sawyer has already proven I can't trust him to stop it. So, to me, that only leaves one option. Like I said, no one leaves the island.

I blink. "You just do."

Lib picks at the loose thread some more, and I watch the comforter slowly unravel. It probably cost over a thousand dollars.

"Thank you," she murmurs, not looking at me. Her cheeks redden, and I lower my eyes to her chest that expands with each inhale.

Her nipples pebble through the silk, and my mind drifts. I feel a tension I know is one-sided, and all I can do is hope she doesn't sense it radiating from me. It's become clear in this conversation what she needs from me. Trust. She needs to trust me.

And I want her to.

"Can you do something for me?" I ask, my voice low.

She raises her eyes but doesn't respond.

"Believe me."

Her head tilts, and her forehead wrinkles.

"I'm not going to bullshit you. I promise. If it seems like I'm trying to sell you on this life, it's because I don't want you to be so afraid of it."

"But *why?*" she asks. "Why do you care how I feel?"

When I don't immediately answer, she continues. "Just be honest with me. Did Sawyer ask you to convince me to do what you people say?"

"No. Sawyer isn't even sure you *can* be convinced." I huff. "And please, stop saying 'you people.' I know what you mean, but I don't like the implication that I'm one of the rapists you seem to be referencing when you say that."

She seems to consider that for a moment, picking at the comforter. "You still haven't answered my question."

I have to think for a second before I realize what she's talking about. *Why do you care how I feel?*

That's a tough one. I hold my tongue, unsure of how much to say.

"Because you're different," I settle on.

Her hands move to rest in her lap. "What do you mean?"

I shrug like I'm unsure, but I've had a long time to think about this.

"I think you're gorgeous," I say, underplaying it. Every woman in this building is gorgeous. Lib is something else. Something magnetic. She pulls me in, and I'm helpless to it. I saw the look in Sawyer's eyes when he first laid eyes on her, and I could tell then that she had a similar effect on him. I'm guessing she's had a similar effect on Julio, and it's cost him his life.

"And you're stubborn." My lips lift into a slight smile. "It's frustrating how stubborn you are, but I also think it works in your favor."

"How so?" she asks, pulling her knees up and resting her hands in her lap.

"I think it helps you get what you want. You don't settle, and you don't negotiate. As annoying as it's been for me when I'm trying to help you, I also like that about you."

"You don't even know me," she says, sounding unconvinced.

I move my gaze over her face and study her uncharacter-istically relaxed expression for a few moments. "I know you a lot better than you think."

Her cheeks turn pink, and she looks away.

I fight the urge to laugh at her embarrassment but allow myself a small smile. "What is it?"

"Sawyer told you about me, didn't he?" she asks, a hint of contempt in her tone.

I gently clasp her chin between my finger and thumb and tilt her head up. "What do you mean?"

She meets my gaze and gives me a look I don't under-stand. "Did he just tell you about me, or did he let you read the messages?"

"What messages?"

"From the chat site," she says, irritation growing. "The one he used to extract every intimate detail about me before plucking me from my life."

My hand, lightly lingering on her chin, tenses. Slowly, I pull away, no intention of responding.

"How does it work exactly?" she asks. "Does he talk to a bunch of different women, weeding through them until he finds one he thinks will make a good fit?"

Yeah, pretty much.

Her nostrils flare, and I put my hand on her knee. Her eyes instantly dart to it.

"You're getting worked up again." I slowly draw my hand back. "Take a breath."

"Just answer me," she demands.

I hesitate but end up sighing with resignation. "Yes, that's how it works. And yes, I've seen some of your messages."

Her eyes remain constricted, but her stony expression cracks. She wasn't expecting me to say that.

"Breathe," I say, reaching out again. She jerks her knee away when I touch it. "If you need to be angry, be angry. But stop letting it get you into trouble. Get your emotions under control so you can get to the women who understand what you're going through. Then you can talk to them."

"What if I never make it that far?"

I pause for a moment. "What do you mean?"

"You act like a good attitude is going to be enough for Sawyer to let me out of this room. Julio made it perfectly clear that isn't the case."

"You think you have to have sex with someone before you'll be let out?" I ask with fake skepticism. In reality, that's exactly what Sawyer will want. He's careful about managing good behavior amongst the women, and a spirited woman like Lib would no doubt create chaos. He won't allow Lib to be with the others until he feels she's properly broken in. She'll need to *prove* she's going to obey. Not just say it.

I don't see that happening.

Lib doesn't humor me with a response.

"What if I told you I knew a way you could be out of here tonight?"

The bridge of her nose wrinkles as she glares at me.

"Not by letting me fuck you."

Her glare softens but doesn't let up fully. "How?"

I glance around the room until I find the closet. I stand and walk to it, hoping Sawyer stocked it instead of just giving Lib one set of clothes. I open the door and am relieved when I see a few items, one of which will work perfectly.

I take the gold, sequin dress off the hanger and walk it over to Lib. She stares at me suspiciously, and when I lay the dress on the bed, she glances between it and me.

"Put it on," I say.

"Why?"

"Because I want you to come to the playroom with me."

"The *what*?"

"Just trust me."

She stares at me like she's trying to see inside my soul while I wait for her to come to the obvious conclusion. If I wanted to fuck her over, I wouldn't need to trick her to do it.

"Why would I trust you?" she asks.

Because I'm willing to kill for you.

"Maybe you shouldn't." I shrug. "But what else are you going to do?"

She bites her lip as she considers this.

"Better question, who do you think will give up first, you or Sawyer? Do you want to know what happens if it's Sawyer?"

She looks away.

"Let me give you a hint… You're not going to be shipped back to your old life."

"I get it."

"He isn't going to send food to this room forever."

"I said I get it," Lib grates out, yanking the dress into her lap.

She glowers at me and points just over my shoulder. "Turn around."

My lips lift into a smirk, but I turn around before she has a chance to see it.

9

LIBERTY

I can feel the vibe of the playroom before we ever enter it.

Voiceless pop music makes my skin vibrate, the sound intensifying as a couple bursts through the set of wooden, double doors. Or not a couple... A man and his victim. You wouldn't know it by the way she beams up at him, stumbling in high heels while hanging onto his arm for support. It's the collar that gives away the situation.

That triggers another thought. Are there non-captives on the island who are okay with this? Is anyone married?

"Don't overthink," Mr. A says, his cinnamon breath hitting the shell of my ear. A tingle spreads down my neck and shoots goosebumps over my shoulder from the sensation, and, frustrated at my body's betrayal, I step away from his touch the moment his hand splays on my lower back.

I turn my head to Mr. A and find him smiling at me with perfectly straight teeth. "I see that brain of yours churning. Just relax. I've got you, I promise."

When he takes my arm, I pull away but follow him to the door. I tug my dress down my thighs, but that just causes cleavage to spill from the top, so I end up pulling it back up. I don't know how he could possibly expect me to relax when he has me dressed up like this. I'm used to the six-inch heels, so I'm able to gracefully walk, but that's the only small comfort.

Mr. A opens the door, the music blowing me back like a gust of wind. I follow him inside, and as soon as my eyes and mind have time to make sense of the place, I regret allowing him to bring me here.

Sex. So much sex. Lights flicker and people crowd the space, bare skin appearing with every flash. The room reeks of sex and sweat, and the sound of voices and groans somehow drowns out the music.

My lungs seize, and my eyes widen. I don't think I can breathe let alone move. If my muscles would cooperate, I'd be running.

Mr. A either doesn't notice or doesn't care because he walks farther into the room without looking back. The doors slam shut behind me, and I whirl my head around. A man in a suit stands next to the exit with his hands clasped in front of him. He doesn't meet my eyes, but I'd bet my life he can sense I'm contemplating running.

But where?

Anywhere but here.

I dart forward in panic when I don't see Mr. A. My shoulder slams into a woman who turns toward me and scowls, but I don't have it in me to pause and give an apology. There are so many people in here, and it's hard to see more than a few feet in front of me, but I hurry forward anyway, my head jerking side to side in search of my 'protector.'

A man with the first few buttons of his black shirt undone steps in front of me, his lips curved up. He touches my arm and leans in to say something, but when I jerk away, bumping into another person, he rears back like I'm the intrusive one.

"Are you okay?" he shouts over the music, but I don't stick around long enough to answer. I hurry around him and let out a sigh of relief when I spot Mr. A up ahead at a bar. His back is to me, but when I catch sight of his blue suit and thick hair, I run toward him.

My eyes bug so that I don't let him out of my sight, and when I make it to him, I grab onto his arm, looking over my shoulder to see if the man from before is following. A sharp exhale flees from my lungs when I don't see him.

"Oh, so you get to touch me, but I can't touch you?"

I snap my head back toward Mr. A, fire burning inside me when I spot the amusement in his eyes.

"What the fuck was that?" I grind out, still not letting go of his arm. We're close enough that if the laws of matter would allow it, I'd meld into him.

"What was what?"

"You said you had my back!"

"*Relax.*" He chuckles. "I have eyes like a hawk. I knew where you were."

I want to glare at him, but my eyes are too busy darting around. I land on a woman in a cage maybe twenty feet from us who's rolling her hips to the beat of the music. She's wearing nothing but a thong, and with the stage lit up underneath her, she's one of the most visible people in here. There are another three stages I can see.

"Don't leave me," I demand, turning back to Mr. A. My voice sounds more desperate than angry, and my heart pounds so hard, I think for a moment I hear it over the noise.

The amusement in his eyes eases as he pries my hands off his arm to turn and fully face me. "No more pulling away from me." He takes my hand and runs his thumb over my skin. I don't dare move. If anything, I wish he'd wrap me in his arms and hide me with his jacket.

This is too much.

Way too much.

If I thought I couldn't live this life before, now I'm certain.

A stunning, middle-aged woman with diamonds the size of boulders in her ears sets two cocktail glasses in front of Mr. A. She meets my eyes, gives me a small chin lift of recognition, then exchanges a look with Mr. A-for-asshole.

"Thanks, beautiful," he says to her, picking up both glasses. He hands one to me and motions toward a row of tables. "Come on."

His large hand claims mine, and he guides me to one of the many tables running along the side of the room. I wring my hands while he drags a barstool over for me to climb onto. Once I'm settled on it, he hovers beside me, standing so close I can feel the heat emanating from his body. I watch his throat work as he takes a sip of his cocktail. Desperate for a jolt of liquid courage, I do the same. My taste buds light up at the sweet vermouth.

It's a Manhattan. My favorite drink.

Coincidence? Or did he know that from my messages? I must've told saltyshells what my favorite drink was months ago. How interesting could those transcripts be?

I don't know, but I also don't care right now. My eyes lock onto a woman whose wrists are tied to two different metal poles that spread her arms apart. She's fully nude, and a man is kneeled in front of her with his face between her legs. It takes a minute for me to recognize the long, flowing, red hair, but when I do, my stomach drops.

"Anna," I whisper. My voice is absorbed by the noise in the room like it never existed, but Mr. A hears me somehow.

He follows my line of sight to Anna, then turns back to me. "Friend of yours?"

Eyes welling, I hop off the stool.

"What are you doing?" Mr. A steps in front of me with a frown tugging down his mouth.

"I have to help her." I try to go around him, but he grabs my shoulders and stops me. I jerk in his hold, but he only digs his fingers in deeper and leans in to talk in my ear.

"*Stop.*"

My body stiffens, and I keep my hands at my sides. His voice has so much authority in it that I actually obey the command.

He lets go of my shoulders and turns us so I'm facing Anna with him behind me. His hands hold my waist like he's afraid I'll try to run.

"Look closer," he commands, his velvety voice softer now, but just as authoritative. "Does it look like she needs your help?"

I stare at Anna while biting the inside of my cheek. The man is still between her legs, and another one stands behind her, fondling her breasts. My stomach flips watching, but I force myself to calm and take in the scene.

Her head is tilted back, her lips parted. Her body doesn't jerk like I expect, but instead, it undulates, her hips rocking against the man's face. I move my eyes back to her face and see her mouth open wider as her eyes slam shut. I can faintly hear the scream she lets out, but it doesn't make me jump toward her because I can clearly see that she isn't screaming for help. She's having an orgasm.

"See?" Mr. A coos into my ear, desire saturating his words. I feel it flowing from the hands on my hips. "There's nothing sinister going on there."

I breathe in the scent of sex, closing my eyes when it's all too much. The heat at my back from Mr. A's body, his hands on my hips, his erection subtly rubbing against me.

I can hear it now. The groans sounding throughout the room are actually moans filled with more pleasure than I've ever felt.

What is going on?

"I want to go," I tell him, my eyes still closed. I open them and spin toward Mr. A. "I want to leave. *Now.*"

"Ivy…"

"*Please,*" I beg, my throat clogging.

He stares into my eyes a moment and must see the turmoil raging in my mind because his face softens with pity as he nods. "Okay." He takes my hand and leads me through the crowd until we're out into the hallway. Light blinds me, and when the doors shut behind us, it's uncomfortably quiet.

Mr. A guides me down the hall and up a flight of stairs. It seems like we walk for a long time before he opens a bedroom door and steps to the side.

"What are we doing?" I ask, hesitant to step through the threshold.

"This is your new bedroom." He gestures inside. "It's okay. Go."

I step past him and am relieved when he follows behind me, kicking the door shut once we're both inside the large bedroom. Six beds total line the walls, only a couple of them made. Women's clothing is strewn about, and the surface of a dresser off to my right is caked with makeup and has a mirror attached to it. A curling iron rests haphazardly on the end, still plugged into a wall outlet.

He guides me farther into the room with his hand on my lower back as I let my gaze roam over the cream-colored walls with magazine clippings tacked to them. When we come to one of the beds, Mr. A lifts a pillow as if to inspect it before tossing it down.

"I don't know if this one is taken, but it'll do for tonight. Sawyer will show you your permanent bed tomorrow."

I squint with confusion and look around. "That's it?" I ask, turning to look at him. "That's all I had to do?"

"*Well*," he drags out the word, "I had intended to stay longer than that, and it would've been nice to find Sawyer so he could see your obedience for himself. But yes, that's it."

I spot an open book, face down on an accent chair. "Are you sure Sawyer is going to be okay with this?"

When he doesn't answer right away, I hold my breath while staring at his blank expression, trying to gauge what he's thinking. I didn't know how badly I wanted to be with the other women until it became a possibility, and now that it has, the idea of going back to that bedroom by myself is suffocating.

I've done nothing for who knows how long, and the thought of returning to that crippling boredom hits me all at once. The book laying on the chair is more tempting than any carrot they've dangled in front of me.

I could read. I could talk to someone other than myself and Mr. A. My eyes drift to a door opened a crack, white tile and porcelain visible through the sliver.

I could *shower*.

"Do you think he will be?" I ask again, trying to keep my voice as indifferent as possible, though the desperation is evident to my own ears.

Mr. A steps up to me and slowly reaches his hand toward my face. He stares me in the eyes like he's waiting for me to jerk away or hit him or something. Before I saw this room, I probably would've. Before I saw Anna come, I *definitely* would've.

I swallow and close my eyes, trying not to hate myself as his hand brushes my hair back behind my ear.

I don't want to fight. Not this. Not right now. Not with him.

So, I stay still, and when he brushes his knuckles over my shoulder, I shudder.

"Do you remember when you asked me if I have much influence on Sawyer?"

I nod, not opening my eyes.

"I do. I can't promise I'll grant all your wishes, but I won't ever make a deal with you that I can't follow through on."

When his touch leaves me, I open my eyes. His expression tells me he's serious, yet I can't read what he's thinking. I lower my eyes, biting my lip when I take in the erection bulging through his pants.

"Take off your shoes."

I hesitate a few seconds, unsure if I really want to go down this road. He clearly wants me. What's the next thing he'll have me take off?

I shudder, the thought both terrifying and exciting. I should be repulsed, but I'm not. He's... I don't know. He's different.

I close my eyes and take a deep breath before stepping out of the heels. They fall over onto the carpet, and I use my foot to slide them to the side.

"Now lay down on the bed," he commands. And he does say it like a command. His voice is stern, full of the authority I heard in the playroom, and although I'm unsure of it or of him, I obey. If for no other reason than my mind is so fucking confused about what to do right now. For the first time since I arrived here, I genuinely am unsure what the best move is. I didn't have to think before this moment. The best move was to fight. To show them they couldn't break me. To prove to *myself* that they couldn't break me.

Now I'm not so sure.

"Under the covers," he says once I'm lying down flat on the bed.

I scoot up and pull the top sheet over me before lying on my back again. I study the ceiling and listen to my heart thump in my ears.

I can see Mr. A out of the corner of my eye, but I can't bring myself to look at him. I know what he wants... I don't know if I'll give it to him.

When he backs up out of view, I turn my head and watch him head on. He pauses at the door before flipping off the light. "Goodnight, Ivy," he murmurs.

He steps through the entryway and clicks the door shut behind him.

10

ANGEL

ind whips through my hair as I look up at the sky while Julio pleads with Sawyer, his hands out in front of him and his back to the cliff. The cold steel of a handgun presses against my back where it's tucked into my waistband.

It looks like it's going to storm. I can smell the rain in the air and can't see a single star as hard as I look, although the moon peeks through the clouds just fine, illuminating the cliff with the help of the bright manor lights a couple hundred yards away. I lower my head to glance between Julio and Sawyer.

"Boss, I swear to you. The bitch is lying."

"Why did she hit you then?" Sawyer asks.

My jaw tightens while I stare at my best friend. It's annoying that he's even listening to this explanation let alone asking for it.

"Because she's fucking crazy! You've been around her. You know. She attacks anyone who comes near her."

Sawyer glances over at me and gives me a look that tells

me he isn't fully convinced of what I've told him. He thinks Lib is lying too. Apparently, Julio has been, "nothing but loyal," and he has, "never been a problem." I don't know if Sawyer has become oblivious or if I'm the one being naïve. It doesn't make much of a difference either way. The outcome is the same.

"Look," Sawyer sighs, rubbing the back of his neck. "Maybe she's lying, and maybe she isn't. Either way, you've gotten Mr. Ramos here pissed." Sawyer drops his hand and looks between us, already extending an invisible olive branch. "I think we can all agree, Julio, that you need to be moved to another position. The boat goes out for another shipment tomorrow anyway, and when you come back, we can sort all this out." Sawyer locks eyes with me and raises a brow. "Fair enough for you, Mr. Ramos?"

No. No, it isn't.

I pull the gun from my waistband and aim it at Julio's head. His eyes widen, but I pull the trigger before he has a chance to say another word. The gun blasts like thunder, which is fitting for a night like this. Julio's lifeless body falls to the ground, and blood drips from the bullet hole in his forehead.

"Goddamn it, Angel," Sawyer grumbles, sounding more angry than surprised.

I walk to Julio's body and aim the gun at his chest. I fire off six shots, an unnecessary amount but enough to ensure that his lungs are fully punctured and there's plenty of blood oozing out for the sea creatures.

I wedge my shoe underneath him before rolling him closer to the ledge. When he's almost there, I shove him forward with my foot then lean over to watch as his body soars to the rocks below.

Once before, I stood at this very ledge, searching for another body below, and when I found it, I cringed. Puked on the ground, my body physically rejecting the horror of that night.

Now I don't even blink.

Sawyer comes up beside me, bristling while leaning over to see. Julio's body has already sunk below the water, but there's a darker patch on a rock, marked with his blood. It'll take a day to fully wash away the evidence. Not that anyone would care.

Sawyer shakes his head and sighs. "You didn't have to do that."

"I told her I would."

"Ah," Sawyer huffs. "Well, then you made the right call. How awful it would have been for you to go back on your word."

I glance at him and frown. "Did you believe him? Honestly?"

Sawyer hesitates, his lip twitching. I don't know if he intends to answer, but his hesitation is enough for me. I've known Sawyer my entire adult life, and I like to think I can read him well.

He knew what occurred. He knew that Lib was telling the truth and that Julio had every intention of raping her. He just didn't care.

"How many times has this happened?" I ask, my chest deflating with disappointment.

His face hardens as he looks out at the ocean. "Judge from your high horse all you want, Angel. You don't understand these girls like I do."

"What is it that I don't understand?"

"Sometimes they need a push."

"So you allow your staff to *rape* them?" I narrow my eyes with a mixture of disbelief and disdain. "That's a weak man's game."

"I *turn a blind eye.*" He enunciates each word, his own

disdain injected into every syllable. "It's rare for a whore to cause so many problems. In situations like these, it takes more than a kind smile and a granola bar."

"She would've had sex with me tonight. Willingly, if I'd told her to."

He scoffs. "Right."

"You don't believe me?"

He's quiet for several moments before he turns to me. "I love you like a brother, Angel. You know that. But sometimes I think you believe what you want to believe. I've been doing this a long time. I know when a girl is ready to give in to her new life and when she isn't."

I nod slowly. "Maybe you're right. Clearly I don't know all your *methods*."

Sawyer's face sags. "You just murdered one of my men in cold blood. Are you really going to give me a hard time?"

I don't answer, and apparently realizing he isn't getting one, Sawyer huffs out a breath and rubs his neck.

"Your girl's safe and sound with the others now. I'm sure she's creating all sorts of trouble for me, and despite my better judgment, I'm going to let her. For you. So … could we please move on from this?"

"No more turning a blind eye," I say. "With any of them."

Sawyer considers this for a moment, then reluctantly nods. I'm disappointed with him. And a little with myself for being oblivious to the fact that shit like that was happening.

This is his island. It's his manor. Our business together is limited to real estate investments and company takeovers. I don't make the rules here, but I thought I at least knew them. Knew *Sawyer*.

I look out at the ocean and take a deep breath in an attempt to ease the tension brewing behind my eyes. "She really would've fucked me," I say, hoping to lighten the mood.

Sawyer laughs. "You sure about that?"

"Mmm hmm."

Sawyer nudges my arm before walking to the cliff and sitting down, dangling his legs fifty feet above the rocks. I follow his lead and sit beside him.

For a minute, we just stare at the ocean. I come here sometimes when I want to torture myself. Like every other time, my thoughts are plagued with unwanted memories, a heavy weight settling onto my shoulders. For a moment, I relive the memory, all of it. I force myself to. There's a certain kind of self-punishment that doubles as comfort.

"You're thinking about it, aren't you?" Sawyer asks.

"No," I lie without pause.

He leans back on his palms and lets out a breath. "Do you remember when we were in college, when we used to hand out incorrect answers to tests so that the curve would be lower?"

I smile at the memory. "Intro to Business."

"Yeah, that was the class. Professor Shizer. God, we were so fucking hated when people found out."

I mimic his pose and nod. "My car was keyed six times that semester."

Sawyer laughs. "But we aced the class."

"I think I ended up with a 98 percent. We probably didn't need to adjust the curve."

"No," he says, his amusement suddenly dying. "You didn't, but I did. You've always been like that, though. It's not enough to succeed, you have to tear down the competition."

My smile falls, and I remain quiet, considering his words.

"Then there was that little Greek restaurant with the best damn gyros we'd ever had. *Still* the best I've ever had." I turn to peer at Sawyer, a look of serenity on his face like he's reliving the memory. "I remember the owner had a cot in the back where he slept. He put everything he had into that place."

I nod, remembering the man. He had a thin, dark combover, and his breath was horrid, but he was a good man. And a good father. His kids would run all over the restaurant, yet I never heard him yell once. When the library kicked us out, Sawyer and I would spend hours at a table in the deserted restaurant studying. The owner never complained.

"It was nice."

"Yeah, it was," Sawyer agrees. "I would've loved to buy it. Throw a fresh coat of paint on it, buy a new sign."

"It could've done well."

"Right, but it didn't." He chuckles, but there's little humor to it. "You were so pissed off when he refused to sell it after we graduated. You put up two Greek restaurants within a couple blocks from the place just to run it to the ground. I remember being so frustrated to watch you take a loss like that on poor investments just to be petty."

Again, I remain quiet.

"You're ruthless, Angel. You want what you want, and you'll tear apart anyone and anything that gets in your way. I love that about you. It makes you a hell of a business partner, and if I'm being honest, I owe this whole island to that side of you. There's no way I could've afforded any of this without the success you've brought us."

"What's your point, Sawyer?"

He picks at a piece of grass, taking his time to answer. "How many men am I going to have to lose before you get this girl?"

He looks up from the ground, and I can see the conflict in his eyes.

"As long as you keep your guys in line, there shouldn't be any more problems."

Sawyer sighs and gives me an 'oh, honey' look.

"What?" I ask.

He shakes his head. "Nothing."

I open my mouth to press him but then close it and let the conversation die.

Sawyer stands and bends to clasp his hand on my shoulder. "Do what you gotta do, friend. Just don't tear me down in the process, all right?"

He doesn't wait for an answer. He pats my shoulder then begins the walk back to the manor.

I stay sitting on the cliff and force myself to relive my memories, telling myself this thing with Lib won't be the same as before. I tell myself I'm a different man, even though I know it's a lie.

When the first raindrop hits my cheek, I finally get up and head to my house.

11

LIBERTY

"Maybe it was firecrackers."

"Firecrackers, Lily? Seriously?"

"Well, maybe they were target shooting or something. Just because we heard a gun doesn't mean anyone got shot."

"Target shooting? At two in the morning? Who does that?"

"Drunk people."

The hushed voices reach me in my sleep, pulling me awake. When I open my eyes, the room is well lit with sunlight. The voices are at my back, so I sit up and turn toward them.

Three women are perched on the bed next to me, and when one's large, muddy eyes lock onto me, she slaps the blonde who opens her mouth to speak.

"Ow." The blonde woman rubs her chest. "What the hell?"

Muddy-Eyes nods toward me, leading all three to turn to look.

"Oh." The blonde's lips lift into a tight smile. "Hi."

"You heard gunshots?" I ask, pushing my messy hair back and sitting up straighter.

Blondie and the third woman wearing black-rimmed glasses exchange a look.

Glasses is the one who speaks. "Last night. There were several after we got back to the room."

"*Lily*," Muddy-Eyes scolds, her condemnation more evident in her bugging eyes than in her voice. "We don't *know* that's what it was. And we're not supposed to gossip."

Someone groans from beneath a comforter on a bed across from us. "Oh my god, would you guys keep it down? Some of us are still trying to sleep."

"Sorry, Molly," Lily whispers toward the hidden woman.

Someone pokes me in the back, and I jump, whipping around while my spine steels. Naomi's sleepy eyes find mine, and I glance down at a blanket and pillow on the floor beside the bed.

"Hey," she says, giving me a smile that's either sad or tired. "Scoot over."

I quickly make room for her and grab hold of her arm as she climbs into bed beside me. The other women whisper, and I'm not convinced it's only out of politeness for those sleeping. I get the sense that they don't want me to hear them.

"Are you okay?" I ask, scanning her as if I could see the emotional scars I know she must have.

"Yeah," she whispers, glancing over me at the other women. She gives me a look that tells me she doesn't want them to hear our conversation as much as they don't want me to hear theirs. "Would be better if you hadn't stolen my bed."

"Shit, I'm sorry." I peer down at the mattress, then back to Naomi. "I didn't know—"

"Hush, I'm kidding. I'm just happy to see you. I would've woken you up last night if I'd known it was you."

"Surprise." I half-heartedly smile. "I'm happy to see you

too. Seriously, though, are you okay? What's happened since I last saw you?"

"I'm fine." Her eyes drift to the other women again. "You need to worry about yourself. Honestly, I'm surprised you're not dead."

"Not quite," I say, half joking.

"Don't trust any of these people, okay?" Naomi's voice is low, and her eyes are cold. "They'll rat on you in a second. Sawyer has almost everyone here brainwashed, so if you're thinking of planning something, don't try to involve them. It isn't worth it."

I hadn't been thinking of planning anything let alone whether I'd be able to recruit any of the women. Before last night, I hadn't been sure I'd even make it up here.

"Okay," I whisper anyway.

"And don't try to tell anyone your real name." Her jaw tightens as she looks at the bed with the woman under the covers. "It's against the rules, and these bitches are more than happy to get you in trouble."

"Really?" I turn my head to peek at the three still whispering. That would explain them not wanting me to hear their conversation.

We're not supposed to gossip.

"Trust me, I learned that the hard way. Just keep your head down and do whatever you're told."

I huff out a breath. "Yeah, okay."

Naomi bumps shoulders with me. "At least for *now*. We can't get out of here if you're locked in the basement, stupid."

Fair point.

I consider it for a moment, then peek at the women again to make sure they aren't listening. "Have you gotten any information that could be useful?"

Naomi shrugs. "Depends on what you mean by 'useful.' So far, all I've gathered is that this is a private island of rich people. We're basically in a whorehouse right now, but if you call it that, they'll get pissed."

"Who's 'they?'"

Naomi nods to the three women. "All of them. I'm telling you, they're brainwashed. Some of them came on their own, but even the ones who didn't look at Sawyer like some kind of saving grace. One girl, Gina, literally told me the story of how he 'saved her.'" Naomi rolls her eyes, but then her face goes serious. "I'm really glad you're okay. I thought for sure the gunfire last night had to do with you."

Blood flows into my cheeks, and I shift on the bed. "I'm not so sure it didn't."

She leans closer to me. "What do you mean?"

I glance around before responding. "Do you know a man named Mr. A?"

"Sure, I've met about four of them," Naomi deadpans. "I'm pretty sure the 'A' is just the first letter of the dude's name. You're going to have to be more specific."

"Tan guy, chestnut hair. Has a slight European accent. Spanish maybe."

Naomi's face stays blank as she waits for more.

"Oh, and he's always in a suit. I think he's a regular at the manor."

Naomi shrugs. "I don't know if I've seen him. Why? What does he have to do with last night?"

A knock sounds on the door, and I jump. Both our gazes move to the entryway just as the door opens and Sawyer steps into the room.

Naomi faces me and leans in to whisper in my ear. "I'll see what I can find out."

I nod before she pulls away and faces Sawyer.

"Morning, ladies," he says, a kind smile on his face. I suspect it's fake, but he's a great actor.

"Good morning!" Lily exclaims. Two others follow her

lead, and the women who were trying to sleep quickly sit up and fling the covers off themselves.

He scans the room until he finds me. His eyes flicker with something that looks like annoyance, and his smile falls when he sees Naomi next to me.

"Ivy, could you please come with me?"

I remain still until Naomi elbows me, and then I begrudgingly climb off the bed and walk to Sawyer, glancing over my shoulder at Naomi as I do. She eyes me with a clear 'don't be an idiot' look.

She's right. I've been handling this situation all wrong. When we were both in the cellar and Naomi started begging to be let upstairs, promising to be good, I tried to pity her, but what I really felt was disgust. It seemed like it took little for her to give up the fight. I'd thought she walked right into the lion's den along with Anna.

But really, she's the smart one. She's been up here gathering what information she could about where we are and the workings of this place, and she's right, I can't help if I'm trapped in the basement.

I need to play along. That's the only way I'll figure out how to get off this island. All I really need is access to a phone, but who knows how long that'll take?

As soon as I get my chance, I'll take it. Until then, the best thing to do is lay low.

I resist the urge to scowl as I make it to Sawyer and peer up at him. I try not to flinch as he slings an arm over my shoulders and turns me to face the other women.

"In case you haven't already been introduced, ladies, this is Ivy. She's had some difficulty adjusting to our lifestyle, so it'd be kind of you all to make her feel welcome."

"Welcome, Ivy." Lily waves, beaming at Sawyer. I want to puke.

I force a small smile directed at Lily. "Thanks."

"'Kay, come on," Sawyer says, turning me toward the doorway. He moves his arm but keeps his hand on my back as he prods me out of the room. As soon as he shuts the door behind us, I jerk away from his touch.

He huffs and shakes his head before he faces the other end of the hall and strides that way. I glance around the empty hallway, not in any hurry to follow Sawyer. He acts just as Mr. A did last night, leaving me as if he couldn't care less whether I come with him.

I bite my cheek and jog after him, slowing to a fast walk as I catch up.

"Where are we going?" I ask.

"You didn't seriously think I was going to be cool with you and April bunking together, did you?"

"Her name is Naomi, and that didn't answer my question."

Sawyer slows to a stop and cracks his neck like he's already had a long day. He closes his eyes, letting out a slow breath, and when his eyes open, there's anger there. He pushes me into the wall and wraps his hands around my neck, not squeezing enough to cut off my air supply but enough to send fear shooting down my spine. My eyes widen, and my lips part.

"Do you want to know a secret, Ivy?"

When I don't answer, his grip on my throat tightens. "Hmm?" My lungs constrict, and panic sets in. He only squeezes my throat for a few seconds, but it's enough to send adrenaline pumping into my veins.

He loosens his hold, and I gasp, clasping his hand and trying to pull it away from me. He doesn't budge.

I bob my head with the little slack he gives me while forcing myself to calm down and put my hands at my sides.

"Yes," I say when his stern glare tells me he isn't satisfied with the nod.

"I don't like to hurt women. I know you probably don't believe that, but it's true. It'd make my job so easy if I did. All it would take is some heroin and a few punches for even a feisty girl like you to fall in line."

"But my secret," he says, leaning closer to me, his eyes as cold as I've seen them, "is that I really, *really* want to hurt you. You had me convinced you were coming around, and I've wanted to fuck you for a long time, but honestly, I'm over that. Now all I want to do is hold your head under water until the bubbles stop. The only thing stopping me is my friend, who still thinks you're fuckable."

When he cuts off my air supply again, my hands fly up to his grasp on my throat. I dig my nails into his hand, but it only makes him squeeze harder.

"But the second your bad attitude bores him," he goes on, "I'm gonna choke you just like this while I fuck you, and I'm going to carry the look in your dead fucking eyes with me as a memento for the rest of my life."

He lets go of me and takes a step back.

I bend over in a coughing fit and try to suck in air. At first, this seems to only fuel the coughing, but eventually, the fire in my lungs goes out, and I'm left bent over with tears running down my cheeks and my hands on my neck as if they could protect it.

"*Or*," Sawyer says, his voice infused with a humorous warmth that was missing ten seconds ago. "You could try not being such a dumb little bitch, and maybe I'll change my mind. Who knows, maybe if you play nice, you and I will even be friends by the time Mr. A is done with you. We'll see."

I watch my tears drip onto the tiled floor. My body shakes, a sob rocking my chest.

I don't dare look up at Sawyer. Until now, he hasn't been the one to hurt me. That was Julio's job.

And now I'm pretty sure Julio's dead.

I didn't think through what the consequences of Mr. A's actions on my behalf would be, but it's crystal clear that Sawyer is tired of me. Or pissed at me. Or hates me. I don't know how deep his negative emotions go, but I believe every word he said.

He's going to kill me.

Another sob barrels out of me, and I flinch when Sawyer takes my chin and guides me to look at him. I stand up straight and suck my lip between my teeth to keep it from trembling.

"Do we understand each other?" he asks, brushing tears off my cheeks with his knuckles.

I nod.

"Good." Sawyer takes my head in his hands and leans in close. "Now… What's that girl's name?"

I swallow but barely hesitate to answer. "April."

A smile blooms across his face, and it strikes me as unusually sincere. Like he finally believes he's won.

He hasn't. Or this round, maybe he has. I'll do what he says right now, and I'll try to, "play nice," but this only makes me more desperate to get off this island. And when I do, it'll be me with the memento.

But for now, I need to focus on staying alive. And that currently depends on Mr. A.

"Good girl," Sawyer says, rustling my hair like I'm a dog.

He steps away from me and points to a door a few feet in front of us. "Your new room. Go before I regret this."

I hurry to the door, open it only enough to fit my body, and squeeze through. I close it and hold the knob with a shaky hand, waiting to see if Sawyer will come in after me. When he doesn't, I let go of the knob and slowly back away, not turning away from the door until my calves hit a bed.

I spin and face another room full of women, this time all staring at me, most wearing curious expressions.

My eyes lock onto another familiar face, and I deflate with relief when Anna's eyes light up.

"Ivy!"

12

ANGEL

I gather the papers for a contract Sawyer and I have been working on for the last hour and a half, and I tap them on my kitchen table to straighten the stack.

Sawyer stands with his hand on my open refrigerator door, surveying the food. He chooses a pear, bites into it, and swings the fridge door shut.

He loudly chews while strutting over to the table where I arrange the papers in the folder.

"I think you should be the one to go," Sawyer says once he's swallowed.

"Not a chance in hell."

"I'm a man short here, and I've got some hiring to do. It'd be irresponsible for me to leave right now."

I lift my eyes from the folder before sliding it across the table to him. "You're not going to let this go, are you?"

"Mmm," Sawyer's lips twist, and he looks up as if he's contemplating it. "Not a chance in hell."

I chuckle at his mocking tone and shake my head. "I've gone the last six times. *Six.* And you're much better with people in these situations."

"By 'situations,' you mean canning people from a job they've worked at for years? Yeah, I doubt they care who's firing them. You hand them their last check, then go on your merry way."

I plant my hands on the table and lean over it as I pretend to hear Sawyer out. We're just about to seal the deal on a string of crummy hotels in Massachusetts called The Charlotte. I visited one the last time I was in the States.

The chain isn't exactly pretty, but the competition is low in several areas, and a remodel would do it wonders. If the owner had the money to redo the flooring and buy some decent mattresses, I suspect it'd double his occupancy. But he can't afford it, which is where Sawyer and I come in.

Some of the people who work there will get to keep their jobs, and the others will always have the option of reapplying when renovations are done and the help is needed. The management, however, has to go. And while firing men with overinflated egos in menial power positions doesn't exactly ruin my day, telling immigrants and single moms they have to find a new minimum wage job to support their families doesn't sit right with me. I come off too direct, whereas Sawyer can somehow make it seem like he's doing them a favor.

"I've thought it over," I say, "and, no. I'm staying."

"We'll both go." Sawyer shrugs before taking another bite of the pear. When he swallows, he sets it on the table and drums on the wood with his hands like he's getting excited. "We can take the jet to New York before we leave and go to that club Gaumond told us about. It'll be fun."

Sawyer and his clubs. This isn't a dance club we're talking about, it's a sex club. You would think the owner of this island would want a change in scenery, but not him. Still, I'd normally be happy to travel together. I don't mind being alone, but Sawyer makes mentally draining business trips exciting. He's always been able to do that.

But I'd rather not leave Lib. It's too risky. For one thing, she could get hurt by another guard or even one of the manor guests. Probably not since the guards know what happened to Julio and why. I'd be shocked if someone tried to pull that shit again.

What I'm really worried about is her acclimating without me. At some point, she's going to get comfortable here. The idea of her doing that with another man sends red hot jealousy through my blood.

"That's an idea." I nod as if I'm considering it. "But I think I'd rather stay. I have a lot of work to do, and you have a habit of distracting me."

Sawyer groans, pushing off the table. "Whatever." He spins around and walks to my liquor cabinet. "Maybe I'll hit Gaumond up anyway. Let him know how his wife's doing."

My jaw tics. I pick up the pear core and walk to the trash can.

"Where the hell is your brandy?" he asks, his head inside the cabinet while he searches.

"You drank it." The pear thuds as I drop it in the can. "And it's ten in the morning."

"I'm on vacation."

"Right."

He pulls out a bottle of gin and grabs two glasses from the cupboard.

"I'm good," I say, picking up the folder.

He looks at me, waving the bottle. "You sure?"

I rattle the folder. "I need to get this faxed over."

"It can't wait twenty minutes?"

I just stare at him.

Sawyer gives me an annoyed expression before he pours a quick shot and knocks it back. He slams the empty glass on the counter and walks my way without putting the lid back on the bottle. I grind my molars together but let the sloppiness go. Two years of rooming with him in college, and I'm still not used to it.

"All right, fine. I'll walk to the manor with you. Buy a new damn fax machine, though. And some brandy."

"I'll put it on my to-do list."

We walk out my back door, starting on the path to the manor. My house sits a quarter mile away from the massive brick building, and Sawyer's sits a quarter mile away on the other side.

When we first moved here, there was nothing. It was a private island Sawyer had the opportunity to buy, and he's turned it into this. I thought he was insane at first, but I was bored with the city life and thought it would be nice to have an ocean view for a little while. Never could I have imagined what the sixty miles of shoreline would become.

"You know you put two of my biggest problem girls together last night?" He tries to come off lighthearted, but his irritation blares through.

"Did I?"

"Ivy and April, yeah. I went to correct the mistake this morning, and they were already scheming together."

My lips lift into a half grin. "How could you know that?"

"I can tell these things, Angel. Don't be surprised if the manor's burned down when you wake up tomorrow."

I chuckle. "Surely you can handle a couple of girls."

"I can if you *let* me handle them."

My smile falls. "What are you suggesting?"

Sawyer glances at me, then watches the ground as we walk. I can tell he's trying to word whatever he wants to say delicately, but his indirectness only irritates me further.

"Nothing. Forget it."

"Sawyer."

"What?"

"She's just a girl. She's not going to burn down your empire."

"Because you say so?" He gives me a pointed stare before relaxing his expression and giving his head a shake. "I don't know... Just forget I said anything. Take care of shit while I'm gone, though. If I come back to a revolution, I'm blaming you."

He faces forward as the manor pokes out above the trees up ahead. When we come to the electric fence, Sawyer punches in the code to open the small gate.

"I'll take care of everything," I try to assure him. "I promise. Everything will be fine."

Sawyer throws open the gate and waves me through. He swings it shut as he steps onto the manor's grounds, gripping my upper arm when we make eye contact.

"I trust you," he says.

A hundred yards away is an inground pool which several scantily clad women lounge around. A speaker by the pool plays American teenage girl music ... the kind that gives you an instant headache.

As we get closer, I spot Lib laid back in a chair with a mimosa resting on her thigh. The redhead we saw last night is in the chair next to her. Desiree, Lily, and Clara are huddled around a cabana table with a fruit platter in front of them.

Lib seems to be the only one to notice us as we approach. Her eyes stay trained on me, but I try not to stare. I wasn't planning on seeing her this early, and with Desiree right there, I don't intend on hanging out.

I nod at Lib as we walk by and am a little relieved when I get nothing in response. When Desiree sees me, however, I'm not so lucky.

"Hey," she says, jumping out of her chair.

Sawyer glances between Desiree and Lib and gives me a knowing smirk.

She smiles politely at Sawyer. "Hi."

"Hey, Des." Sawyer gives her a chin lift.

Her eyes move back to me. "Could I talk to you in a bit when you're not busy? Just sometime before you go home. It's not that important."

I open my mouth, an excuse as to why I can't do that balanced on the tip of my tongue, but Sawyer cuts in.

"He's not busy now." Sawyer flashes his freakishly white teeth as he takes the folder from my hand. He tips it at me and backpedals a few steps toward the rear entrance. "I'll take care of this."

"Thanks," I say, my lips stiffly tilted up while my eyes tell him to fuck himself.

"No problem, brother." He spins and walks inside, but not before giving me one last shit-eating grin.

I turn to Desiree. "What's up?"

"Why was there gunfire last night?" she whispers like it's a secret from the others.

I flinch back a hair like I'm puzzled. "Gunfire?"

"Yeah, around two. You don't know what I'm talking about?"

I pretend to think about it for a few seconds, scratching my temple. "It stormed last night. You probably heard thunder."

She shakes her head. "No, I'm certain it was a gun. You really don't know?"

I shrug. "I haven't heard anything."

"Okay." She glances down, nodding like she's accepting it. Her eyes fly back to me, and her lips part. "You know I'm not trying to gossip. I'm just concerned for our safety."

I almost snort at that.

"I know it's against the rules to kill slaves and everything, but…" She leans in close and glances at Lib. "Honestly, I thought it might've been that girl."

"Like you said, that would be against the rules."

"Right, but—"

"You're safe, Des. Is that all you wanted to talk about?"

She opens her mouth, and her eyes dart to Lib again before she speaks. "So did you ever find that girl last night?"

"Ivy? Yes."

"And?"

"And what?"

Desiree huffs like she's exasperated by my cluelessness, but she quickly composes herself. "*And* what happened? Why did Sawyer want you to check up on her?"

"I thought you weren't trying to gossip."

"It isn't gossip," she says, waving the idea away with her manicured hands. "I just… I mean, I'm curious, you know? You say you're going to make sure some girl who's been nothing but defiant is acclimating well, and then she winds up sleeping with the rest of us that same night. I can't help but wonder what could've led to that happening."

Her tone is hard, and although she doesn't come right out and say what's on her mind, the accusation is clear.

Annoyance flares, but I stifle it enough to keep it from showing. There was a time Desiree had the ability to make me jealous too. "Are you asking me if I fucked her?"

She doesn't say anything, which is enough of an answer for me.

"No, I didn't. But it wouldn't be your business if I did."

She looks equally relieved as she does hurt, and I instantly want to call back my words. A month ago, I gave her a good chunk of my time, and now I give her none. I get it, I've sent some mixed signals. I'm probably an asshole, but there's only one woman I'm now interested in, and she isn't Desiree.

I lighten my tone and relax my face. "You're aware there's no romantic connection between you and me. Right?"

Her face falls, but she recovers and gives a slight shrug. "Yeah."

"So then it would be inappropriate for you to ask me who I have and haven't slept with. Right?"

"I was just curious."

"Don't be," I say, my voice a little too sharp despite my efforts. "I don't want you to get in trouble for gossiping. You know how Sawyer feels about that."

Her disappointment seems to morph into resentment at my sarcasm. Her ruby red lips purse and her arms cross over her chest. "Thanks for looking out, pal."

I open my mouth but bite my tongue and decide to let the remark go. Most men on the island would have her thrown in the cellar for her shitty attitude, but—lucky for her—I'm not a fan of punishment. In fact, I'm starting to notice I like sassy women. Just not Desiree.

I glance at the door and turn that way. "See you later, Des."

"Yep. Bet you will."

I don't bother responding to that one either. I steal a quick peek at Lib before I head inside, finding her fully turned in her seat, her eyes darting between Desiree and me.

I face the manor and slip through the door.

13

LIBERTY

I watch Mr. A as he walks inside the manor, then my eyes move to the clearing he just came through.

"God, I love this song," Anna, or *Annie*, says. Pretty sure Sawyer thought it'd be cute and clever to name her after Little Orphan Annie. Which, as much as I hate to tip my hat to him, is fitting.

Miley Cyrus blares out how she, "came in like a wrecking ball," and Anna sings along.

I turn toward her and lean her way. "Hey, do you know what's over there?" I ask, tipping my head toward the clearing the men appeared from.

"Hmm?" She sits up and removes her sunglasses, pushing back her hair.

"The clearing over there." I point that way. "Where does it lead?"

"Hmm," Anna hums, this time as a verbal ponder instead of a question. "I don't know."

I stare that way and tap on the arms of the chair.

"We could ask Sawyer," Anna suggests.

I take a steady breath and turn to meet her eyes, the corners of my mouth tilting up slightly. "No, that's okay. I was just curious."

She lounges back and takes a sip of her mimosa, going back to the clueless bliss she's trapped herself in. I hate to think this way, but I don't trust Anna. I'm taking Naomi's warning seriously, especially after my encounter with Sawyer. I can't imagine Anna having a malicious bone in her body, but I still think she'd run to Sawyer if I prodded her too much.

Still, she's all I have right now.

I nurse my drink as I look around the courtyard. It really is a magnificent property. Born and raised in the city, I've never seen so much green in one place. There's a huge garden down a ways with a sculpture of some saint and an impressive arch at the entrance. There are so many types of flowers with ivy climbing up stone and wooden structures, it'd be the perfect place for privacy.

"Want to take a walk?" I ask Anna.

Her eyes are closed as she basks in the sun, but at my voice, she squints at me. "Where?"

"Maybe in the garden. It's beautiful."

"Oh, um, sure." She puts her glass on the concrete patio and stands, adjusting her skirt in the process. I follow her lead, but neither of us move as the blonde from this morning walks up to us.

"Hey," she says, smiling. Freckles dotting her nose barely show beneath her skillfully-applied makeup, but they become more visible when her face scrunches and she uses her hand to shade her eyes from the sun. "Where are you guys headed?"

"We're going on a walk in the garden," Anna tells her. "Wanna come?"

"I'd love to." She looks over her shoulder at the two women she's been sitting with. Both stare at us.

"But actually, Annie, I think Margarette was needing some help in the kitchen. Could you go? I was on kitchen duty last night."

"Oh." Anna looks at me, and I shrug. She turns back to the woman. "Yeah, sure."

"Thanks. See ya."

Anna gives me one last look before heading inside, tossing a farewell over her shoulder with a wave of her hand.

"Ready?" the blonde asks me, her smile too hard. I glance at her friends, then back to her. She's been fifteen feet away from me for the last hour, yet all I've gotten from her were daggers. I've been making a mental list of women I may be able to trust and women I definitely can't. She's already been put into the 'definitely can't' column.

Just a few minutes ago, she pulled Mr. A to the side, though. Did he ask her to do something?

"Yeah," I say, because what else am I supposed to do?

We start toward the garden, and I flinch in surprise when she interlocks her arm with mine like we're in the third grade. She turns to change our direction, looking over her shoulder like she wants to make sure no one is noticing us. I look too and am not at all surprised to see her friends still staring.

I try to pull my arm from hers, but she locks me in tighter and guides us toward the side of the manor. "Let's walk down the beach instead."

When we turn a corner around the manor and are out of her friends' sights, she lets go of my arm.

"What are you doing?" I ask.

She flips her hair off her shoulder and tosses a glance my way. "Saving your ass."

My eyebrows raise, but I school my expression after the

slip. She couldn't possibly know what I was about to do … could she?

"What do you mean?"

"The garden has cameras," she says, sounding mildly annoyed. "They would've heard everything you had to say."

My mouth goes dry as I curse myself.

"Yeah. If you really want privacy, you have to go to the beach. Every spot on manor property is too dangerous."

"Including here?" I ask, searching the tops of the stony exterior walls.

"Yes, but there's probably no audio here, so just walk like we're pals taking a stroll. Quit looking for the cameras."

I face forward and swallow.

"I'm Desiree, by the way."

I glance at her and give her a slight introductory nod. "Liberty."

"You mean Ivy?" She fixes me with a stern look. "Don't get caught saying that around here, hun. You'll have bathroom duty for life."

"Right, I meant Ivy." I face forward, mentally transporting back to this morning. Desiree is sugarcoating it… I'll have a lot worse in store for me than cleaning toilets if I'm not careful. Plus, I already determined this woman is untrustworthy. "Sorry," I mutter.

"Hey, don't apologize to me. I don't give a shit what you call yourself, although I have to point out, Liberty is ironic as fuck."

I let out a laugh intended to be dry but surprise myself when there's a trace of humor in it. This is the first time I've laughed since stepping foot on the island. "That thought has occurred to me as well."

"Point is, I'm not a rat. I just think you should be careful who you say things to."

I nod. "April's already warned me of that."

"And yet there you were, trying to pump Sawyer's new pet for information."

I look over at Desiree and dip my chin. "Anna?"

"*Annie*," she corrects, emphasizing the last syllable. "Jesus, you suck at this. But yeah, her. Surprised?"

My lips stay parted as if I am, but I know I shouldn't be.

"Fuck," I mutter under my breath.

"Yup. Close one. You're welcome."

I'm silent for a few moments while I try to wrap my head around this. It's starting to make sense why Sawyer bunked Anna and me together.

"Why are you helping me?" I ask, my voice low.

She doesn't miss a beat, like she was waiting for me to ask. "Because a year ago, I was exactly where you're at. Trying to think of every way I could escape, finding out all I could about the island. I've just been biding my time until someone like you came along."

My steps falter, and I have the urge to stop altogether and spin her to face me, but I remember the cameras and keep walking.

"Surprised again?" she asks.

"Very."

I completely misjudged this woman.

"Figured. Now shut up until we hit the beach."

I press my lips together as we walk up to the gate I climbed over my first day on the island. Today, a muscular guard with a crew cut—I think his name is Austin—stands with his back against it.

"'Sup, my favorite Aussie," Desiree calls out, flashing him her pearly whites.

He lowers his chin as a greeting then points at me. "She's not allowed out."

We stop in front of him, and Desiree looks at me then back to him with a puzzled expression I almost believe is real. "I just asked Mr. A five minutes ago if it was cool if we took a walk on the beach, and he said yes."

That's what she was talking to him about?

No. She's lying to the guard. Right?

I'm having a horrible time reading this woman.

Austin doesn't speak, but I can see the uncertainty pinching his face.

Desiree huffs like this is the biggest inconvenience of her day, then starts to turn. "Hold on, I'll go get him. Jeez, you guys are so untrusting."

"Hold up," Austin says, already opening the gate.

Desiree winks at him as she passes through. "Thanks, baby."

I blink, stunned by her brazenness, and nearly forget to follow. I stumble after her, heavy metal banging behind me as Austin shuts the gate.

I have to speed walk to match her pace as we walk down the sidewalk in front of a row of boats toward a sandy beach that stretches as far as I can see. Once I'm caught up to her, I lean in. "Were you telling the truth?" I ask in a hushed tone.

She smirks at me. "About Mr. A giving us permission to walk the beach? No. That guy's an asshole who doesn't give a shit about us enough to go against whatever Sawyer wants. But he's a *scary* asshole, and the guards don't like to take a chance on pissing him off."

My stomach churns, but I try to not let what she said about him going along with what Sawyer wants paralyze me. Him going against what Sawyer wants is what's keeping me alive.

"What were you talking to him about then?" I ask.

We spot a man in his boat up ahead, so we keep quiet until we're safely past.

"What was I talking to who about?" Desiree asks.

"Mr. A."

"Oh," she exclaims like she wants to slap her forehead and say, "duh."

We step onto the beach, and my flip-flops kick up sand. I pause to take them off, and Desiree does the same.

"I wanted to know what the gunfire was from last night, and he took that as an opportunity to scold me for gossiping. Like I said, he's an asshole."

"Oh." I consider telling her my theory on what that gunfire was but decide against it.

"You'd think sucking the guy's dick for the last year would be enough for a little bit of intel."

I'm mid-bend to pick up my shoes when her words cause me to falter. I take several seconds to recover, but finally hook the straps with my fingers and stand up straight.

Desiree stares at me with an intense look that makes me think she's eager for my reaction.

I continue down the beach without offering a response. My eyes stare straight ahead but catch Desiree watching me from the corner of my eye.

"I need to warn you about something," she finally says when I don't take her bait.

I glance her way and wait for her to go on.

"I'm pretty sure Mr. A is going to do the same thing to you that he did to me. Keep in mind, if he found out I was telling you this, he'd probably strangle me, so please don't tell anyone I'm saying this."

There's a tremor in her voice that makes her fear contagious, and the knots in my stomach tighten. I turn her way to give her my full attention, but all I really want to do is bury my head in the sand and pretend this conversation isn't happening.

Up to this point, Mr. A has been the only tiny, minuscule speckle of light in what is otherwise a completely dark society of creeps. He's been more like a savior to me than anything else, and I could go without hearing his sinister motives. I know they're there. I'm not stupid.

But a girl can hope.

"I won't say anything. I promise."

She takes a deep breath like she's readying herself for something. "So first of all, have you slept with him? I'm not trying to get in your business, I just have to ask."

"No," I say, images of the lust in his eyes when ordering me to lay down in bed flashing in my mind.

"Good." She lets out a sigh of relief. "Do yourself a favor and stay as far away from him as you can. If he sinks his teeth into you, there's no going back. He's dangerous with a capital D, despite what he presents to you."

"I don't understand," I say, confusion bleeding into my tone. "What do you think he wants with me?"

"He wants you to be his slave."

When I stop walking, Desiree slows her steps and turns toward me. She looks up to the hill behind us and sits in the sand, facing the ocean. I slump down beside her and watch a speedboat zoom in the distance.

"Sawyer said I was a manor whore."

"You are. That's exactly where Mr. A wants you."

I turn my head toward her, and she gives me this pitiful look when she sees my confusion.

"He probably isn't even after you, so I don't know why I'm telling you this," she says unconvincingly. "I just took him asking about you last night as a red flag."

"He asked about me?"

She nods. "When we were in the playroom. He was looking for you. He said Sawyer wanted him to check up on you, but I think that was a lie."

After my morning with Sawyer, I agree with Desiree's judgment. Sawyer most definitely didn't benefit from Mr. A checking up on me last night, and I have a hard time believing he sent someone to be kind to me.

"I've seen him do this before. He takes an interest in a new girl for a little while, makes them think he's somehow different than the rest of the pricks on this island, then he gets bored and moves on to the next conquest. He's been playing this game with me since shortly after I got here."

I wish I didn't believe her. I wish all this sounded like bullshit and didn't make any sense, but what she's saying is eerily similar to Sawyer's words, and I believe it.

So that's what I am to him. A conquest.

Of course. What else did I expect?

"Why would he do that?" I ask, trying not to sound disappointed.

Desiree tucks her hair behind her ears and folds her legs beneath her as she faces me. "I don't know for sure, but I think it's because he likes the close connection. He isn't allowed to own his own slave, so he uses whatever manor whore he's interested in that second as a surrogate. The majority of the masters here don't keep the same slave long-term, so him getting bored isn't shocking." Her face falls, and she looks down at the sand. "I guess I was an idiot to think it might've been different with me, huh?"

"No," I say because it seems like it's what she wants to hear. In reality, I don't understand why she wants that. What, is she in love with the guy? Who cares if he moves on to the next? Good riddance.

Except I'm doing the same thing, aren't I? I need him not to move on from me. My life depends on it.

"H-how long does it usually take for him to get bored?" I ask.

A divot forms between her eyes, but she must realize it because her face softens as she clears her throat. I'm picking up on some jealousy from her, and if I wasn't currently fighting for my life, maybe I'd be able to conjure some sympathy. But she's quickly putting herself into the same category as Anna in my mind.

"Does it matter?" she asks. "He isn't going to rape you, so all you have to do is just blow him off until he moves on. I think we're getting another shipment soon, so you won't have to wait long."

Shipment? Did she just call human beings a shipment?

"You haven't even asked the important question," she adds, a hint of annoyance cutting through her warning.

"What?" I blink.

"Don't you want to know why he isn't allowed to have a slave?"

I nod, although I'm not so sure I do.

"He killed his last one."

My eyes would widen if my face hadn't turned to stone. My lungs constrict as I turn toward the ocean, staring out at one of the most serene views from one of the most disturbing places.

Whatever hope I had of using Mr. A as a shield falls apart and slips between my fingers.

"Believe it or not, the masters have rules too. And not killing slaves is one of them. Even Mr. A isn't immune to that one."

"When did this happen?" I ask weakly, afraid to know the details.

"A few years ago."

I pull my knees up and press my forehead against them, closing my eyes and smelling lavender lotion.

"Don't worry." She pats my back. "Sawyer won't let him seriously harm you. You should stay away from him, though. You know ... just in case."

I laugh dryly and shake my head. "Mr. A is the only thing stopping Sawyer from killing me right now."

Oh, the irony.

"What?" she asks, genuine confusion in her tone.

I lift my head and squeeze my eyes with a blink to ease the burn coming on. "Sawyer told me this morning he's going to kill me as soon as Mr. A loses interest in me."

"Oh my god..." She faces forward, her eyes darting around as she thinks.

"I have to get off this island." I say the words out loud even though I meant to say them to myself.

"Yeah," she agrees, her voice just as quiet. She turns to me and grabs my arm like she just had an epiphany. "I can help."

My eyes go wide. "What?"

"Get up." She raises to her feet, dragging me with her. Swiping her shoes off the sand, she walks quickly down the beach, so I grab my shoes and hurry to keep up. My ears heat, and I look around like someone can read my thoughts, but there's no one in sight.

We walk several minutes before Desiree stops and plops to the ground. She pats the sand beside her, and I sit.

"There," she says, craning her neck toward a hill behind us. "Through the trees, there's a building. Don't look too obvious."

She faces the ocean and raises her chin like she's sunbathing. I don't know who's benefit it's for, but I follow her lead, then as inconspicuously as I can, I turn and search for the building she's talking about. I can just barely see the top of a structure poking over the treetops.

"That's enough," she says.

I face the ocean again.

"That's the crematorium. It's where they, well ... you know, with dead bodies."

My heart gallops. "I thought you said they weren't allowed to kill slaves."

She raises a shoulder. "Shit happens. Sawyer can do whatever he wants. It's the island inhabitants who have to follow his rules, but I know they still get passes in the right circumstances. I mean, you notice Mr. A wasn't kicked off the island or anything."

I take a sharp breath.

"No cell phones are allowed on the manor premises, and it would be a waste of effort to go for the one phone there is since it's located in Sawyer's office. It's monitored more carefully than the Mona Lisa. You have to go off the property to get your hands on one, and I think there's an office phone in the crematorium."

I force myself not to look at the crematorium again, my blood pressure spiking. The hope I watched slip through my fingers is suddenly shoved into my face, begging me to grab it. And to think, an hour ago my plan was to be a good girl. Forget that.

I can do this.

I can fucking do this.

"The front gate is guarded at all times, so you'll have to take the path you watched Sawyer and Mr. A take earlier. That's where it leads. There's a separate gate that needs a passcode for you to get through. It's 59843."

I repeat the numbers several times before asking, "How do you know all this?" Part of me wonders why she hasn't already done this herself, but I understand. I'm *terrified*, and I haven't had enough time to fully absorb the consequences of getting caught.

"I watched Mr. A type it in. Like I said, I've basically been his slave for the last year."

My nose wrinkles. He took her to a crematorium? I decide not to bother asking about it. I'm wasting time, questioning everything she tells me. She's right… I have a habit of asking the wrong questions.

"When is the best time to go?" I ask instead.

"Tonight, when everyone is in the playroom. They can't keep track of all of us then."

"But the guard," I say, remembering the man blocking the door last night.

"Let me take care of that." She gives me a devilish grin. "I know how to work these guys. It'll be easy to distract whoever is working the door."

My insides feel like they're buzzing, this plan fueling me with adrenaline. I don't know how I'll be able to wait.

"Just hang out by me, wait for my signal, then leave casually like someone requested you somewhere else. It happens all the time, so it shouldn't be a problem."

She must read the terror-filled determination on my face because she puts her hand on my knee for comfort. She inhales a shaky breath and wipes underneath her eyes, like there are tears there that I can't see. "I can't tell you how glad I am that someone like you showed up here. You're not just saving yourself. You're saving all of us."

That thought should put a mountain of pressure on me, and it does add some, but it also eases the dread gnawing at my insides when I think of waking up another day in this hell. After my conversation with Sawyer, I have every reason to lay low. It's what the reasonable part of my mind is begging for. Do what they say and survive, just like Naomi is doing.

But what would I be waiting for? Death? A life of forced servitude, tending to the needs of countless, disgusting men with overinflated egos? This isn't just my life on the line, like Desiree said. There's another boat coming, and if I can get to that phone, I can spare whoever is supposed to be arriving from this horror. I could save everyone.

I push my fear down as far as it'll go, and I square my shoulders. Even if I don't succeed, it'll be worth it.

At least I'll be able to say I tried.

14

LIBERTY

Desiree was true to her word.

All I had to do to leave the playroom unnoticed was wait for a group of three—one man and two women—to walk out the door. I followed right behind to blend in with them, and with Desiree talking up the guard, he never even cast his eyes my way.

I broke away from the threesome—pun intended—and am now almost to the back exit. I plant myself against the wall next to a sliding glass door, inching my head far enough out to peek.

Two couples play chicken in the pool. A woman I haven't seen around the manor yet screeches as she falls off the shoulders of a muscular man with a long beard. They laugh as she comes up for air, flinging her hair behind her. She splashes the others with a smile on her face.

A circular, inground hot tub is only a few feet from the corner of the pool, and it's occupied by Sawyer and Anna. His hand grasps the back of her head as they kiss while she straddles him. Apparently, Desiree was right about them too.

I look past the pool toward the break in the trees as I try to come up with a plan to get there without anyone seeing.

I can't go out the front because it's heavily guarded. I could go upstairs to one of the balconies and try to climb down, but I risk running into someone along the way.

I nibble nervously on my lip and peek outside again.

Sawyer's busy. As far as I can tell, his eyes aren't even open. The hot tub and pool are illuminated, and there's one patio light on, but it's still relatively dark.

I move my gaze to the other two pairs.

Would they notice me? Maybe. Maybe not. They're busy too.

I don't recognize either of the men, and I know the women aren't from the manor because they're wearing collars, which is something I've learned only personal slaves wear. So if they saw me, would they even be suspicious? They don't know my history.

I draw in a deep breath and look up at the ceiling, my toe tapping along to the beat of my racing heart. I decide to go for it. If I get caught, I'll pretend to simply be avoiding the playroom, which isn't a bad idea anyway. I spent an hour in there, feeling more exposed in the skimpy, black lingerie—required by Sawyer—than if I'd been naked.

I slip out of the unnecessarily tall heels and pick them up with a finger hooking each one. After one more deep breath, I gently slide the door open just enough for me to squeeze through the gap. I plant my toes onto the cool concrete with a delicacy that's more fitting for entering freezing cold water.

No one looks my way.

I move my whole body outside, ease the door shut behind me, and speed walk along the patio, my shoulder brushing brick as if my new home will shield me.

My eyes point toward the grass, all my focus on getting

there. It feels like it takes an eternity, and I expect at any second for someone to yell out at me or for a spotlight to blind me, but the splashing and laughs continue, and I never hear my name.

When I step onto grass, I finally throw a look back at the pool. The two women sway on the men's shoulders and flail their arms to try to shove the other into the water.

I break off into a sprint toward the tree line, my heels swinging in my grasp, and don't look back until I've safely made it to the clearing. I crouch and peer at the people, my chest heaving from running with panic. I nearly laugh when no one notices me.

I shuffle backward, then stand up straight once I'm out of sight.

The gate Desiree told me about comes into view, and I take the dirt path toward it. I hold my breath while typing in the passcode she gave me, my hands shaking so badly the heels jostle. When I hear a buzz and the gate unlatches, I let out a rush of air.

I slip my shoes back on, but the heels dig into soft earth as I make my way down the path, so I ditch them and continue on barefoot.

I squint into the darkness, only the stars lighting my way. I make it maybe a minute before a stick crunches under my foot, and I stumble.

"Shit," I wince, bending to inspect my foot. I rub the sole and feel nothing but dirt, so I don't think the skin is broken.

It starts to feel like I've been gone a long time, so despite now having to hobble down the path, I pick up my pace. Every few seconds, I look over my shoulder, half-expecting to see Sawyer chasing me.

My breaths are loud and shallow, and when I make out the building Desiree told me about up ahead, a victorious yelp bursts from my mouth.

Hope floods me and sends tears to my eyes. I hurry to the building, no longer concerned with my foot.

I'm surprised by how big the structure is. It doesn't at all look like the sinister crematorium I pictured in my mind, more like someone's home. There's a back patio with a table and firepit which is also suspicious.

Am I at the right place?

I look up ahead but don't see any other buildings. Would Desiree really have overlooked this? Maybe it's not just a crematorium. Maybe that part is in the basement.

I search for a lit-up window but don't see one, so I walk to the sliding glass door, reminiscent of the one I just went through, and I tug it open.

My feet touch tile, and in the tiny bit of natural light that illuminates the place, I make out that I'm in a kitchen. I search for a light, and when I flick it on, more confusion sets in.

It's definitely a house.

I frown as I walk past a kitchen table and into a living room.

"Hello," I call out, twisting my head side to side to see if someone will jump out of the shadows.

No response. Good.

I step into the kitchen in hopes of finding the door to the basement, still convinced I'll find what Desiree told me about. I swing it open, flip on the light, then descend the steps. Bottles of wine lining a shelf come into view, and my frown deepens. It's just a wine cellar.

Something's wrong. I'm not in the right place.

Why didn't Desiree tell me there was a house along the path?

An uneasy feeling forms in my stomach as I make my way back upstairs, but I don't lose hope. No one's home, and there could still be an office here.

There could still be a phone. Or a computer. Or *something*.

I make my way through the kitchen and living room before trying a door down a hallway beneath the staircase.

Bathroom.

Next door.

The knob doesn't turn.

That's a good sign, right?

I jiggle the knob and throw my shoulder into the wood, but it doesn't budge. I haven't explored the entire premises, so I decide to come back to this room later.

My feet carry me up the stairs where I find a large bedroom, probably the master. There's a door off to the side that I'm guessing is the bathroom, but that isn't what catches my attention.

On the nightstand beside a king-size, four poster bed is a cell phone plugged into a charger.

My eyes widen, and I inhale a sharp breath. I sprint to the nightstand and jerk the phone off the charger. When I swipe to unlock it, it asks for a passcode.

Immediately, my fingers tap frantically on the screen, trying to find the emergency call button. But I think twice about it... We're not in the United States, so who exactly would it call?

I search for the emergency call anyway but don't find it. Can you disable that feature?

"No," I whine, tapping in useless numbers for the passcode. I do this five more times before it locks me out. I groan and lower the phone, throwing my head back to look at the ceiling.

Think, Lib. Think, think, think.

The phone has an owner. The owner will be back.

What if I sneak up on him? I could get a knife from the kitchen or a heavy object to hit him over the head with. I could force him to give me the passcode, then...

Then I'm free.

All it'll take is a phone call to Robert, and help will be on the way.

But what about in the meantime? My chest constricts. I'll still have to get back to the manor without anyone noticing I was gone ... which means I'll have to somehow bind the owner of this phone or kill him.

Am I capable of killing someone?

For my freedom, probably.

I toss the phone on the bed and turn to go downstairs to get a knife from the kitchen, but I pause, deciding to get a blunt object first, then a knife.

I turn back around and pull the lamp shade off the lamp. I jerk the cord from the wall then toss the whole thing on the bed. I could probably cut the cord for the lamp and use that to tie the guy up. That could work.

I open the nightstand drawer, intent on rifling through the owner's things just to cover my bases, but my hands freeze and my jaw drops when I lock onto the magnificent piece of metal.

Gingerly, I grasp the handle of the gun like it'll go off if I anger it. It's heavy in my grasp when I lift it up, and I rotate the barrel while studying it. The hope from earlier swells until I feel like I'll burst.

I won't need the knife after all.

15

ANGEL

Once again, I can't find Lib.

My eyes scan the playroom, coming up empty again and again. My patience wanes with each passing minute.

I check my watch, my jaw sore from grinding my teeth. I've been here thirty minutes already with no sign of the only reason I came tonight.

I drag my hand over my jaw, then take another drink of whiskey. Once my glass is empty, I'm giving up. I don't even think she's in here, which means Sawyer neglected to tell me *again* that she wouldn't be with the other women tonight. Another night wasted.

I rake my gaze over the playroom, out of pure delusion at this point, and spot Desiree headed toward me. One more reason to be pissed at Sawyer.

I down the rest of my whiskey and slam the glass on the third table I've migrated to tonight. I turn toward the exit and head that way before Desiree can reach me.

"Mr. A!" she yells over the music. I keep walking.

"Hey, wait!" I don't wait.

I meet tonight's guard's eyes and lift my hand to gesture for the door. He opens it, and I exit the playroom, but not in time to stop Desiree from barreling through the doorway and crashing into me.

Whatever was holding my patience together snaps.

My shitty mood tonight isn't her fault. I tell myself this in my mind, but it isn't enough to stop me from spinning around and grabbing Desiree's gaudy, thick chain necklace. I grasp it and yank her toward me, watching shock take over her expression.

"Enough," I growl. The door slams shut, and silence engulfs us. "We've had fun, but learn to take a hint. I'm not interested in you anymore. Stop chasing after me, and stop pulling me to the side. Just fucking leave me alone, all right?"

I let go of the necklace, and she stumbles back, hurt replacing the shock on her face. It's enough to sober me, and I consider apologizing, but I don't. I swear to God, if I have to dodge this woman one more time, I'm going to lose it. Even more than I already have.

"I'm sorry," she says, her voice uncharacteristically small.

I turn to leave before guilt has a chance to fully settle in, but she follows after me. She actually *follows. After. Me.*

"I wasn't pursuing you," she tells my back, sounding surprisingly sincere. "I'm worried about Ivy."

My steps halt, and I turn to her, folding my arms in front of me. "What about her?"

What looks to be even worse pain twists Desiree's face. "I knew you cared about her," she whispers, shaking her head.

"Why are you worried, Desiree?"

She blinks a few times and pulls back her shoulders. It looks like she's preparing herself to speak again, and finally, I see the woman I know. Desiree isn't one to show her vulnerability. She's more the retaliate-with-over-the-top-cattiness type.

"She isn't in the playroom."

No shit.

"And today…"

I tap my thigh impatiently. "Yes?"

"If I tell you, you have to promise not to tell on me."

I resist the urge to roll my eyes. "'Kay."

"*Promise* me."

"I fucking promise. Could you please just spit it out?"

She takes a deep breath, and a flash of worry comes over her face. "Today, after you and Sawyer went inside the manor, Ivy went to go check out the gate. I followed to see what she was doing, and she started talking about trying to escape tonight."

She inhales dramatically like she's revealing this deep secret. I'm not the least bit surprised to hear this, but worry does start to nip at me.

"Did you tell her the fence is electric?"

Desiree nods. "Yeah, but she already knew, and somehow, she found out the passcode."

"Shit," I say, my eyes going wide.

"I know. She's been pumping people for information nonstop all day, so she must've gotten it out of someone. I think it was Summer."

Summer. I find that hard to believe, but it's possible. She's a trusted manor whore who cleans my house sometimes. It could be several people, though. Admittedly, I'm not that secretive about the way to access my house. I regret that now.

"I don't care who it was," I decide out loud. "Why didn't you tell anyone about this sooner?"

Desiree frowns. "Because I know the consequences for her if I did. And I took her to the beach and had a really long talk with her about it. She promised me she wouldn't try anything."

I sigh and close my eyes, running my hand through my hair as I do. I don't fault Lib for trying to escape her fate. I get it. Part of me even likes that she's been so difficult to cage. Most of me even.

But I'm growing very tired of the way she's going about things. Her attempts are useless. She's nowhere close to getting what she wants, and she doesn't even know it.

"Where would she have gone?" I ask, letting my hand fall to my side.

Desiree shrugs. "Your house, I think. She talked about trying to find a phone. I don't think she was planning on actually running. She's not quite that stupid."

I catch the indignation in Desiree's tone but ignore it.

I turn and head for the back exit.

"What are you gonna do?" she asks, hurrying behind me.

"I don't know."

"Do you want me to go get Sawyer?"

"No," I snap, jerking to a stop. I spin and face her. "You *do not* tell a soul about this, do you understand?"

She nods, and I force my face to soften. "You did the right thing by telling me. Now go back to the playroom and pretend this conversation never happened."

I pause a moment, debating on apologizing. I'd prefer things to be tense between us, but I also don't want her getting pissed off and running her mouth to someone just to spite me.

"Sorry about earlier."

She stares at me, resting bitch face on full display. I turn to leave without either of us saying another word.

When I get outside, several people are by the pool. A frequent manor guest, Alec Crow, waves and calls my name, but I ignore him and stride toward the gate. It's so dark out, I can barely see in front of me as I travel the path to my house, but I could walk it blind with muscle memory at this point.

It takes several minutes to reach my back door, and I have a moment of relief when I don't see any lights on inside. Maybe Lib didn't go through with this ridiculous plan after all.

I throw open my sliding door and step inside. Before I ever get the light on, I hear a click, and my eyes dart to the left. Even in the dark, I can clearly make out my gun held steady in Lib's hands.

"Turn on the light," she commands.

I'm taken aback for a moment, but my surprise quickly turns to anger. "What's your plan here, Ivy? You going to take me hostage?"

"Turn. On. The. Light."

I huff out a laugh and hold out my hand. "Give me the gun."

"Turn on the fucking light!"

My jaw clenches, and I slowly lower my hand, flexing my fingers when it's at my side. I use my other hand to reach for the wall and flip on the kitchen light.

Lib squints like she's been in the dark a while, and I wonder just how long she's been hiding out here, waiting to point my own gun at me.

I inhale deeply through my nose to steady myself.

"Unlock the phone." She nods toward the table where my cell is. I glance between it and her. She rocks back and forth on her heels, hinting at the endorphins flowing through her veins. Her eyes are wild, and both her hands hold the gun tightly enough her knuckles have turned white.

I give my head a shake. "What the hell are you doing?"

"Just do what I tell you," she practically yells. "Otherwise, I'll shoot."

"Will you, though?"

I watch fear flicker across her face, and for a brief moment, I think it might drown out the sheer power she must be feeling. Fear and power… That's a deadly combination. I wonder what she's more afraid of, getting caught or shooting someone.

"Yes," she says, a disturbing amount of certainty in her tone.

"Wow." I pick up my phone. "That's cold. Especially considering how much I've helped you."

She laughs dryly. "Don't talk about helping me. You've been trying to make me your surrogate slave, you sick fuck."

My jaw tics as I hold up the phone. "Who exactly are you planning on calling?"

She doesn't answer.

"You understand 9-1-1 doesn't work here, yes?"

"Unlock the phone and stop talking."

I glance between her and the phone again before letting out a heavy sigh. I don't believe her when she says she'd shoot me. I think she's a lot of things, but I seriously doubt she's capable of murder. Even if she was, she would still need me to unlock the phone.

The gun rattles in Lib's newly trembling hands. Her fear is starting to take hold, and I imagine she's figuring out just how fucked she is. How fucked she *could be* if I hadn't made it to her before someone else. I've never been more grateful for Desiree insisting on coming to me with the manor's drama.

I could take the gun. I'm certain of it.

But something's stopping me. I'm tired of her fighting me. I'm tired of her pathetic attempts to resist her new life. I could wait for her to come to terms with things and accept them on her own, but her recklessness is growing, and I'm running out of patience. She needs a push, and this is my chance to give it to her.

If she manages to use a phone, whether mine or someone else's, she'll call Robert. Sawyer told me that the day she got here she was begging a passerby to call her husband. I bet she views him as a big, powerful protector, with all the right connections and enough money to get to her within hours.

I could take the gun. Let her beg me for forgiveness, then comfort her while she cries in my arms. She'll either be grateful for my mercy or she'll hate me for stealing her false chance at freedom.

Or I could snuff out her hope once and for all.

I look down and unlock my phone.

"Here." I hold it out for her. "Make your phone call."

Her eyes tighten like she suspects I'm up to something. She's hesitant, taking in the phone like it's a piece of cheese on a mouse trap. Just like the mouse, she can't resist. She reaches out and snatches the phone from me.

"Back up," she commands, her voice deceptively strong.

I hold up my hands and back up several steps. "You can put the gun down. I'm not going to stop you."

The gun rattles more now that she's holding it with one hand, so I step out of the line of the barrel, just in case she accidentally pulls the trigger. Her gaze flits between me and the phone as she dials, her eyes not staying trained on me until she presses the phone to her ear.

* * *

Lib

I NEVER KNEW a dial tone could be so loud.

Every time it sounds in my ear, I jump a little, as if I'm surprised it's there. My heart beats against its cage, and the gun feels slippery in my sweaty embrace.

Mr. A stares at me with an expression far too calm for a man with a gun pointed at him. He looks like he knows something I don't, making me wonder which one of us has the false confidence.

After the fifth dial tone, the phone picks up, and relief engulfs me.

"Hello?" my husband's sleepy voice caresses my ear in the softest embrace, and tears spring to my eyes. I'm speechless for several moments as Robert sighs into the phone.

"It's five A.M. here. Can whatever this is not wait?"

"Robert," I say, my voice cracking.

For several seconds he's silent, and I picture him just as speechless as I was when I first heard his voice.

I can't tell you how many times I've questioned my love for him, always believing I deserved better, never appreciating the life he gave me. Not anymore. In this moment, I've never loved the man more.

"Liberty?" he asks, sounding rightfully shocked.

A sob bursts from my mouth, and I close my eyes, forgetting for a moment that Mr. A is watching me. I rehearsed this in my mind so many times, and this was never what I imagined. I planned to be calm and collected. Efficient. Waste no time.

"Baby, is that you? Are you okay?"

"No," I say, shaking my head even though he can't see me. I struggle to draw in a full breath. "Th-they took me." I gather what saliva I can in my dry mouth and swallow. Finally, I find my voice. "I'm on a private island, a man named Sawyer has me. I don't know his last name, but I spoke to him on a chat site. You should be able to track him down through his IP address if you dig into it. H-his username is saltyshells123."

"Jesus, Liberty," Robert says. "I'll call the authorities."

"Hurry." My voice splinters again, and I look away when I meet Mr. A's pity-filled eyes. Pity-filled. Not fear-filled. Not the eyes of a man about to go to prison.

"Don't worry, honey, help is on the way. I have to hang up now so I can call them."

"No!" I nearly double over. "Use the office phone. Please don't hang up."

"I'll call you back," he says, his voice reassuring. "I promise. Just stay put, okay?"

I close my eyes as tears spill but snap them open to focus on Mr. A, gripping the gun tighter.

"Honey?"

"Okay," I say.

"I love you."

"I love you too."

The line dies, and I lower the phone with a shaky hand. I stare at Mr. A while a weird kind of fear paralyzes me.

It's strange how hope works. When it feels like you have nothing, hope can make you brave. But then when the hope is real, when you see the safety on the horizon and you're so close to touching it, it's the most terrifying thing in the world because suddenly, there's a chance of losing it. Losing everything.

"Why do you look like that?" I ask Mr. A.

He arches a brow. "Look like what?"

"Like I'm the one who should be pitied." I wash my gaze over him. "You're about to go to prison for the rest of your life."

He says nothing. Doesn't move a muscle or even blink.

"My husband's going to find me."

Mr. A slowly nods. "I'm sure he won't have to look very hard."

Goosebumps sprout over my arms.

What does that mean?

We stare at each other as a minute goes by and then another. I glance at the phone every few seconds.

"He isn't going to call you back, Lib."

Lib.

Not Ivy. Not Liberty. Lib.

Lib?

My stomach clenches like someone's making a fist with it in their grasp. "What are you talking about?"

He cranes his head toward the phone. "Call him back and put it on speaker."

The fist tightens. "Why?"

"Just do it."

I glance down at the phone and question what's taking so long.

He's talking to the authorities. That takes time. It hasn't even been that long.

Right?

"Sawyer's going to be here soon." Mr. A frowns and waves to the phone again. "Do it."

I chew on my lip as I bring up the recent calls, searching for my husband's number at the top. But I don't see his number.

I see his name.

Nausea overwhelms me, and I swallow down bile. I click on the name and put the phone on speaker, watching as the hope within my grasp slips farther away, like I'm walking backward.

My hand shakes profusely, and I nearly drop both the gun and the phone when Robert answers on the second ring.

"Liberty?"

"It's me," Mr. A says, taking a step closer to the phone.

"Jesus Christ." Robert sighs, this time with relief. He lets out a little laugh. "What happened?"

I lower the gun and stare at the phone with tears blurring my vision.

"Your wife's feisty." Mr. A takes another step toward me.

Robert laughs again. "You don't say?"

"I don't know how she managed to unlock my phone," Angel says.

"She's a resourceful little bitch."

I flinch like he slapped me. A slap would've hurt less.

"She is," Mr. A agrees. "Sorry about waking you. I'll let you get some sleep."

"Don't worry about it. Hey, call Sawyer, though. I just got off the phone with the manor, so he's probably looking for you."

More tears leak onto my cheeks as I look past Mr. A out the sliding glass door. Flashlights shine in the distance, getting closer by the second.

"Will do. Thanks."

Mr. A closes the distance between us before gingerly grasping the phone.

"And hey," Robert's voice is full of amusement. "Give my wife a kiss for me."

Mr. A takes the phone from me and hangs up.

Once again, I'm speechless, but for an all new reason. My chest hurts like my heart has literally broken as I stare at the lights getting closer and closer.

When Mr. A goes to take the gun, I jump back a step and lift it, pointing the barrel at his chest.

He raises his hands. "Come on, Lib. They're almost here. You need to give me the gun."

"Fuck them," I say, my gravelly voice barely above a whisper. I turn the gun toward the door, ready to fire at the first person to come through.

I'm not quite numb, but I feel like I'm underwater. I can feel the heartbreak, the betrayal, the agony, but it doesn't quite settle inside me. It's a force on the outside, suffocating me until I can't think straight. I can't make sense of anything.

He knew.

He *knew*.

Not just that...

He *gave me away*. Didn't he?

No.

No fucking way.

No fucking way is this my life.

"Hey, look at me," Mr. A says.

I move my eyes to him, shattering even more at the sympathy he so clearly displays on his face. Sobs erupt from my chest, and his mouth contorts into a frown.

"I know," he tenderly says, as if he could possibly even fathom what I'm going through. "But it's going to be okay. I promise."

Something about the way he says this takes a sledge-hammer to my already decimated pieces. I still can't process things. I can't figure this out right now.

Men arrive at the door, and Mr. A steps in front of me, shielding me from their view. "Let me help you." He reaches for the gun again.

I stare at his hand, watching numbly as it grasps the gun. I don't know how he can help me. I don't know how he can make things okay.

But I let go anyway.

He opens a kitchen drawer, tosses the gun inside, slams the drawer closed, then opens his arms for me.

Men file in through the door, guns drawn, and I press myself into Mr. A's chest, seeking sanctuary in his embrace.

Sawyer's voice is the first that I hear.

"What the *fuck* is going on?"

ANGEL

I throw a look over my shoulder and meet Sawyer's eyes when his angry voice hits my back. I try to turn, but Lib latches onto me so tightly, I'd be dragging her if I did move. Her face is buried in my chest, her entire body trembling.

"It's okay," I coo, petting her head.

I go to turn again, and she inches with me this time, her feet shuffling almost comically on the tile.

When I meet Sawyer's eyes again, his anger is evident, his upper lip curled back and his eyes blazing. "She got ahold of your cell phone," he sneers, as if I don't already know. "Why are you coddling her?"

I skim over the three men with him, all with their guns still drawn.

All this for a 120 pound woman.

I motion to the men. "Call off the dogs."

"Angel…"

"It's *fine*. I'll explain everything once we're alone."

"I'm not leaving that bitch by herself." Spittle flies from his mouth as he talks, like he's caught rabies or something.

I've never seen him so angry, and it almost makes me regret allowing the phone call.

But no, she needed that. I'm certain of it.

Instead of arguing further, I stare back at him and wait. Part of me starts to question if he won't pry Lib from my arms to throttle her.

Sawyer's mouth is set in a hard line while he stares me down, but eventually, he concedes and waves off the men. They put their guns away and start toward the back door.

"Don't leave," he says to them. "Stand outside and guard the doors."

"Yes, sir." I can't help but grimace at the one who looks like he's about to salute. He's the last to leave, and he stands so tall it's annoying. This isn't the marines, kid.

Once they're gone, I take Lib's shoulders and slowly push her off me. She raises her head to peer at me, and the look she gives is clear enough it doesn't need words attached to it.

Help.

"You're fine, just wait here."

"We're not leaving her alone," Sawyer reiterates. "Whatever excuse you're about to make for her, you can do it here."

I lift my gaze to him. "Would you calm down?"

"Calm down?" His eyes widen, and he takes a step toward me.

Lib seems fully aware of his proximity, and she moves behind me, using me as a shield.

"I'll calm down as soon as this cunt is buried. She *contacted* someone. That goes way beyond the manor rules, that's a rule for every slave on the island. She's dead. Period. Don't fucking try to convince me otherwise."

"I made her call Gaumond."

Sawyer stiffens like he's turned to stone. "What?"

"I wanted her to see for herself that there's no escaping. She's been held back by hope that her husband is going to save her, and I thought it would be beneficial for everyone if she knew he wasn't."

"If she had called anyone else…"

I raise a brow. "I watched her dial. How could she have called someone else?"

He closes his mouth as he thinks about that. I didn't realize how much I'd have to lie to get him to calm down about this.

Sawyer glares behind me, his nostrils flaring. "I'm *done* with this bitch's bullshit." He shakes his head. "Either take her or she's dead."

"I can't have my own slave."

"I don't fucking care!" Sawyer clenches his fists then unclenches them to run his palms over his face. He drops his hands and glares at me. "Choose. Death or yours."

Choose.

Not a suggestion, not a request, a command. A use of power. Against *me*.

Is he out of his fucking mind?

Something primitive inside me takes over, and all rational thought goes out the window. I try to remember this is Sawyer. My closest friend since college. My brother. The person in my life I care about most.

But I can't see that right now. All I see is an enemy, a challenger. I raise my chin and step up to him. He doesn't budge, clearly feeling up to the challenge.

"Did you just give me a command?" I ask, my voice muted yet full of ice.

His jaw works as he stares me in the eyes. "You're not gonna put this on me any longer, Angel. Be pissed. I don't care."

"You're not killing her."

"You're not bringing her back to the manor."

"Would you rather I take her home?"

His eyes darken. "Excuse me?"

"Well," I drag out. "We both know me keeping her as a slave isn't an option. Killing her is also not an option. So if you're saying you're not willing to budge on the manor, the only solution I can see is to take her back to New York. Give her a lump sum of money to start a new life, Robert Gaumond free. I'm sure she wouldn't *dare* go to the authorities." My lips tilt at my own sarcasm. I turn my head to the side to address Lib, but I don't take my eyes off Sawyer. "Would you, sweetheart?"

"No," Lib breathes, so much hope in her voice I feel bad for saying all of this in front of her. Of course it isn't an option.

But at the same time, if Sawyer doesn't loosen the fuck up, I may make it an option.

Setting Lib free could hurt me. If she went to the police—which let's be honest, she would—it could lead to giant payoffs and favors owed to who knows how many people, not to mention the fact that I wouldn't be able to have her, which is obviously unacceptable. And I'd lose my brother, which is also unacceptable.

But Sawyer? Sawyer would drown in the anxiety. He'd be looking over his shoulder for the rest of his life. He'd use every dollar he had to track her down, and even after he found her, he'd question if she told anyone about the island. He'd literally go insane.

As the possibilities play out in my mind, I realize just how right he was during our conversation the other night. If I can't get what I want, I'll take a hit to burn my opponent's goddamn world to the ground.

"You know I can't let you do that," Sawyer says, sinister meaning dripping from each word.

"How exactly could you stop me?" I tilt my head. "Do you think you have it in you to kill me, Sawyer?"

His jaw tics again, and I can't help the tiny smirk that lifts my lips.

"You wouldn't do that." He shakes his head. "You're not that stupid."

"No, but I'm ruthless, remember?" My smirk lifts even higher. "You can't possibly believe you can come into my home and bark orders at me without retaliation. You know that doesn't bode well with me."

Sawyer breaks eye contact and stares at the wall like a defeated teenager who's just been grounded.

"You're angry," I continue, ensuring that my voice displays compassion I don't feel. "Go home. Sleep on it. Ivy will stay here tonight, and you and I can talk about this more in the morning, when we'll both be able to think rationally."

He returns his gaze to me then takes a step back. "Fine." He glances behind me at Lib then back to me. "We'll talk in the morning."

I nod. "Looking forward to it."

Sawyer glares another few moments before turning around and heading for the exit. He pauses in the doorway and looks at me over his shoulder. "I think it goes without saying, but I'm not going to be the one leaving the island right now. You're handling Massachusetts."

Yeah, I figured.

He doesn't wait for me to so much as acknowledge his words before he storms out.

As soon as he's gone, I turn to Lib. "I need to say something before you speak."

She backs up into the sink, no longer using me as a shield. Now *I'm* the threat.

Two steps forward, one step back.

"You're not going home," I inform her, my voice level. "I'm sorry if you truly believed that was an option, but it isn't."

She nods. "I know."

When a tear leaks onto her cheek, she brushes it away. Her whole body continues to shake.

I take a step toward her. "Are you okay?"

She slowly lifts her chin up and down, but then she closes her eyes and shakes her head.

I close the distance between us and take her in my arms. I hug her as she cries, her tears wetting my shirt.

"It's okay," I say, injecting as much reassurance into my voice as possible. "You're okay. Nobody's going to hurt you."

She lifts her head to meet my eyes. "That's not true." She croaks out a sob like her body's rejecting her words. "Sawyer told me he would. He said as soon as you're tired of me, he's going to kill me."

"He won't." I smooth her hair back and tuck it behind her ear. "I'm not going to let him hurt you, I promise."

"I'm not going to try to run again," she says, hugging my shirt. "I swear."

I smile slightly. "I know."

"I don't even have anything to run back to anymore."

"I know that too."

And I do know. I know her so much better than she thinks. So much more than even Sawyer is aware of.

Her lip quivers like she's about to start sobbing again, so I take her face in my hands and lower myself so I'm inches away.

"This is going to be okay, Ivy. I promise you. As soon as you quit fighting, it won't be nearly as bad as you've been imagining it."

She closes her eyes and whispers her next words like she's afraid of saying them out loud. "I don't want to die."

I frown. "I know you don't. You're not going to."

"How can you be so sure? What if Sawyer doesn't cave tomorrow?"

"Do you think *I* will?"

She opens her eyes and studies me. I don't think she's even taken into consideration what I might do. She's too terrified of Sawyer, seeing him as this higher power that decides all, just as most of the other inhabitants see him. Which is true, in theory.

"I have an idea," I say, caressing her cheek. Her skin is so smooth, it makes it easy to forgive the commotion and stress she caused this evening. I'm enjoying this. Her not pulling away. Her seeking safety in my arms.

"If it will make you feel better, why don't you join our conversation tomorrow? You can tell him everything you're telling me."

Her teeth graze her lower lip, and she takes several moments to answer. "Okay."

"Come on. We can talk more in the living room. If you want." I take her hand, and she lets me guide her to my living room sofa. She doesn't seem to register it as she drops down onto the cushions. Her eyes are glossed over, staring into space like she's deep in thought.

I walk back to the kitchen where I pour each of us two fingers of whiskey. Once back at the couch, I hold a glass out to her which she gingerly takes. I freeze, my own drink inches from my lips when she downs the whiskey in two gulps. Her face twists as it burns her throat, and her lips are still puckered when she sets the empty tumbler on the coffee table.

I sit next to her and go to put my hand on her knee but think better of it, resting it on the back of the couch instead.

"I know you," she says, not looking at me but peering down to where she fidgets with her hands in her lap.

Finally.

"We met when Robert and I were dating." She picks at her cuticles. "I didn't remember until Sawyer said your name."

I keep my mouth closed because I'm not sure what to say.

"It was at a charity event. It was the first one I ever attended, and I was nervous as hell."

I stay silent, still unsure how much I want to tell her. I knew it was a possibility that she would recognize me, and in all honesty, I was disappointed when she hadn't. But I never planned to tell her what I remember. Or how much I know.

"You gave me your last cigarette. And your friend was an asshole."

I watch as she puts the puzzle pieces together.

Her eyes bulge. "That was Sawyer, wasn't it?"

"Probably," I say, deciding not to confirm nor deny her recollection. "He and I travel together often. And he's an asshole."

She blows out a halfhearted laugh and leans back against the cushions, studying the ceiling. "How could he do this to me?"

"It isn't personal." It never is. "You're beautiful. And intriguing. A little more so than he bargained for, but that's what initially made you desirable to him."

She shakes her head. "I don't mean Sawyer, I mean Robert. He sold me, didn't he? How could he do that?"

I hesitate to answer, not sure how to respond.

Lib was a trophy for him. She looked nice on his arm. She cooked his meals, washed his clothes, and sucked his dick. She's no more a slave here than she was there. There was never any *true* love, not on his side, at least.

That's the real reason she's here. She's lustworthy and has proven to be loyal to a man who doesn't love her. This should've gone far more smoothly.

I don't say these things, though. It's all true, but the truth hurts. Lib is already devastated.

"I don't know," I say instead.

"How could *you*?" she asks, leaning toward me while she

waits for my response. She isn't asking me this out of anger like she has in the past. She isn't lashing out at me. She genuinely wants to know.

"I'm not a good man."

She looks down at her hands again. "You lied to Sawyer to save my life."

"Because I like you. It wasn't a selfless act, it was for my benefit."

She's quiet for a beat. "You're so strange."

I don't fight the chuckle that bubbles from me. "Am I?"

She glances at me then back to her hands. "I was told about how you sometimes take a special interest in new women. I just can't believe you'd take it this far. It's honestly weird that you're not letting Sawyer kill me."

What?

"Who told you that?" My eyes strain in confusion while I try analyzing my actions to figure out how someone could've come to that conclusion.

I don't like new girls. Not interacting with them, at least. For one thing, they're always skeptical, of me in particular. For another, I don't get off on fear or anger, nor do I ever want to force a woman to do something against her will. It's the reason I haven't already had sex with Lib, even though I saw a chance before. Hell, I see a chance *right now*. You can get someone to do anything when they're fearing for their life. That's easy. And weak.

She looks up at me. "Does it matter?"

I consider this. No, I guess not. I guess it doesn't even matter if she thinks that's what this is.

"How long does it usually take you to move on to the next?" Unable or unwilling to maintain eye contact, her eyes float between her hands and me. She speaks again before I have a chance to respond. "I'm not asking that out of judgment, I'm asking because I want an honest idea of a timeline.

I'm going to try my best to get on Sawyer's good side by the time I'm not so intriguing to you."

I shake my head. "You have the wrong idea about me."

I study her face and can tell she isn't convinced.

"Who have you been talking to?"

She doesn't respond.

"Ivy…"

"I don't want to get anyone in trouble. I just want you to be honest with me."

I take a deep breath and speak evenly. "I don't have a timeline."

"How long was the last?"

"The last what?"

"The last conquest." She peeks at me. "Again, I'm not judging. I just—"

"Six months."

Her lips part as though she wants to say something, probably argue with me about my own life, but it's my turn to interrupt her thoughts.

"I was in college, there was this cute girl who worked in a coffee shop. I flirted with her for a month before she agreed to go out with me. We dated for six months after that."

Lib's forehead wrinkles like she's confused.

"The women I've fucked on the island didn't need some grand effort from me. I've only been with the ones who are here because they want to be here. They aren't conquests, they're just people."

"What about Desiree?"

Annoyance floods my system just from hearing her name, and my mind reels back to earlier. Desiree said she had a talk with Lib today.

Oh, Jesus.

"She's the one who's been talking to you about me, isn't she?"

Lib folds her arms over her stomach. She doesn't respond because she doesn't need to.

I roll my shoulders and blow out a frustrated breath. "Desiree is going to tell you whatever she needs to so that you'll stay away from me. She's jealous of you, that's it."

Lib shifts her position so that she's facing me.

I sigh. "She and I had a little fling in the past, and I regret it deeply. I'm pretty sure I'm *her* conquest. I'm not sure if she truly wants me or if she just can't stand the idea of someone not wanting her."

Lib blinks, an emotion I can't read crossing her face.

"If you want real honesty, I remember you from that charity event too. Also, I've heard plenty about you from your husband over the years. You aren't some random, new whore to me. I know who you are, and I do genuinely want you to be okay. And yes, I find you intoxicatingly desirable, and I very much want to sleep with you. But this isn't some fetish. I—"

"Is there a crematorium around here?"

I close my mouth and feel my brows pinch.

"Is there one?"

"You mean like at a funeral home? Why?"

"Please just tell me."

I pause for a moment, wondering where she's going with this. "No."

"You swear?"

I don't bother responding. I just stare at her and wait for her to explain what the hell she's talking about.

"Oh my god." She scrubs her hands over her face.

"What's wrong?"

She shakes her head.

"Ivy?"

When she doesn't say anything, I prod her again, and finally she looks at me.

"This was a set up."

One brow raises. "What?"

She blinks. "I mean, I did this. It's my fault I'm this naïve. But today, Desiree made it seem like any minute you'd drop me... Or kill me. She told me this was a pattern for you, that you did the same to her. And before I talked to her, Sawyer said he's just waiting on you to get tired of me so he can kill me."

Goddamn it, Sawyer.

"Okay," I drag out the word. "So what? You felt like you were fucked either way, so you had no choice but to sneak into my house and steal my gun?" I can hear the sarcasm in my voice, and I regret it. She either doesn't notice or doesn't care.

"I mean, yeah, but more than that, Desiree told me this was a crematorium that had a phone in the office and that she'd been waiting for someone like me to show up so we could save everyone. If she hadn't told me that, I wouldn't have..." Fresh tears begin to fill her eyes.

I sit as still as I can, sure if I move, I'll snap. It takes all the willpower I have not to storm to the manor right now and throw Desiree against a wall. And yet I'm not remotely surprised she'd try to do this. But I *am* surprised she was sly enough to pull this off. Maybe she isn't as dumb as I thought.

"How could I be so stupid?" Lib mutters to herself.

"Did she give you the code for the gate too?"

Lib nods.

Fucking bitch. She sent me after Lib, knowing what it could mean for her. Like I said, I don't often go against Sawyer. And this is a crime worthy of death.

She wanted Lib dead.

I could kill Desiree. It scares me how badly I want to.

But I won't. I already have more than one ghost haunting me.

Lib laughs dryly. "God, she even told me you killed a woman."

My chest seizes. I'm taken back to the night, feeling the sweat on the back of my neck, the humidity in the air. I feel the anger, but most of all, I feel the regret, see the body flat on the rocks. I close my eyes and focus on my breathing.

"I can't believe she'd do that," Lib whispers.

I open my eyes, doing my best not to show the turmoil churning my insides.

I should tell Lib what happened before someone else does. Everyone knows I'm a murderer. Hell, *she* knows I'm a murderer. She knows what happened with Julio.

Someone's bound to tell her about Beth.

I look at Lib as I debate over this in my head. If I don't tell her and she finds out, she will no doubt never trust me. But if I tell her now … how would it turn out any differently?

It wouldn't.

But still…

"She wasn't lying about that," I admit, my voice surprisingly even.

Lib looks at me. "What?"

I take a steadying breath, feeling my face harden. "Years ago, I had a personal slave. She was a woman Sawyer met in The States, and he talked her into coming to live on the island. I bought her six weeks into her being here, and we lived together for a year."

Lib slouches, but I can tell she's trying not to look affected by what I'm telling her.

"And … you killed her?"

I'm quiet for several seconds, searching for words that can adequately describe what happened. But there's no version where I'm innocent. I know that. It doesn't make a difference for Beth if I feel badly or not. She's still dead.

"Yes," I finally answer. Lib flinches, and I almost do too.

My voice is too cold. It's like my mind won't allow me to show the utter weakness I feel inside. "It wasn't by my hand, but I drove her to commit suicide. We weren't a good match, and we both knew it. I should've realized how unhappy she was, but I didn't, and one night we were arguing by a cliff. I ended up storming away, and when I came back a half hour later, she'd already jumped."

I don't mention how I found Beth's body caught on a rock, mangled and bloody. By the time I could get to her, the tide had pulled her body into the ocean, and she was found days later by some people on a yacht. It's a night that'll haunt me for the rest of my life, and the worst part is, that was history merely repeating itself. Beth isn't the only person whose life I've destroyed, and hers isn't the only mangled body that haunts me. That's a longer list.

"Most of the inhabitants assumed I pushed her off the cliff, and a couple of the manor whores even claimed they saw it happen. I never disputed it. Suicide or not, I'm the reason she died." My tone hitches, but it's nearly imperceptible. I sound firm and unapologetic, like I'm simply taking responsibility for a misfortune. What an asshole.

"And that's why you aren't allowed to have your own slave."

Not a question, but a statement.

"Yes. It's an island rule, but more than that, it's mine." I look across the room at a useless shelf, holding nothing but decorative shit meant to take up space. "I don't trust myself with that kind of responsibility."

"And yet," Lib sounds cautious, choosing her words carefully, "You expect me to trust you with my life."

Fair point.

"Unfortunately for you, I'm all you have."

Lib chews on her lip while she digests that. After an

excruciating amount of time, she speaks. "I'm really tired. Would it be all right with you if I went to bed?"

"Of course," I say. "There's a guest bedroom upstairs. Second door on the left."

She gets up and heads upstairs without looking at me or saying anything. I don't blame her.

I pick up my glass and watch her go. Once she's out of sight, I pour the whiskey down my throat and stand to get more.

It's going to be a long night.

17

———

LIB

I keep my eyes trained on Angel's kitchen table but can feel Sawyer's stare burning into me. His skepticism is so potent, it's like there's a cloud of tension hanging over the room that coils my muscles until I feel like my back's about to snap.

Angel stands a few feet away from me, his arms crossed casually over his tan, bare chest as he leans against a counter. Sawyer stands at the opposite end of the table, staring down on me like a deity. Neither man sits out of fear of losing the high ground.

"I don't believe you," Sawyer says at last. I've been waiting on him to speak for a solid minute, but it could just as easily have been five hours.

Angel didn't prepare me for this, and I wish he would've. I wish I knew the right words to say to Sawyer instead of just, "I'm sorry," or, "I promise I'll behave." I've exhausted those at this point. Meanwhile, Angel just stands watching us, saying nothing. I don't know what exactly I expected him to do, but I'd hoped he'd do at least some of the talking.

I take a shaky breath. "I understand." My eyes finally lift

to meet Sawyer's. "I probably wouldn't believe me either. But *please*, give me one more chance."

Sawyer's head tilts. "Why would I do that?"

I glance at Angel, but his expression remains impassive. I try to implore him with my eyes, and he either doesn't get my message or doesn't care.

My eyes find Sawyer again. "Because Angel wants you to. I get that what I want probably doesn't matter to you at this point, but—"

"*Angel?*" A muscle jumps in Sawyer's cheek, and his eyes bulge. Despite saying his name, he isn't speaking to Angel. He's speaking to me.

I shrink away from the sheer contempt in Sawyer's glare, and again look to Angel for help.

He clears his throat. "I'm still Mr. A to you, Ivy. You aren't allowed to use the first names of island inhabitants living outside the manor."

"She isn't allowed to *know* first names." Sawyer's scowl moves to Angel.

Angel scowls back. "You're the one who gave it to her."

Sawyer's expression softens, confusion evident in his eyes.

"Last night, you called me by name."

Sawyer thinks for a moment then swears under his breath.

"Sorry, I meant Mr. A," I say.

Sawyer moves his eyes to me.

"I won't call him by name again."

He doesn't look at all convinced, and I can understand why.

My heart is beating so fast, and my palms are getting sweatier by the second. It feels like there's a massive lump of iron in my chest.

I'd say anything right now to take away the murderous look on his face.

But I do mean these things. I'm not lying to bide my time. I'm not scheming in my head. Honestly, I'm just trying not to fall apart. I'm trying to survive.

And my hope of ever leaving this island? Yeah, that's dead. Fucking. Dead. Not just because I'm terrified to try again but also because of who my husband is and what I know he's capable of. All the connections he has and then all the connections these people must have.

I thought Robert was powerful enough to get me out of here, but he's also powerful enough to keep me from getting out. I can already hear him telling the police some fabricated mental health history. See him playing the part of the doting husband, concerned for his wife's sanity.

The police won't help me. Robert won't help me. That leaves no one. Naomi was right all along... I'm fucked.

"Please," I say, closing my eyes and lowering my head. My voice breaks, but no tears fall. I'm all out of tears.

Another eternity passes while Sawyer contemplates ending my life.

"Is she really worth this?"

I open my eyes and peek over my lashes. Sawyer has turned toward Angel, his arms crossed over his chest.

Angel peers at me, then back to Sawyer. "Yes."

"But you were bluffing last night, right? You wouldn't actually try to take her off the island."

Angel just stares at him.

"I'm *sorry* for giving you a command, all right? I was just pissed."

Angel nods. "I know."

"Then fucking work with me here."

Sawyer's voice holds a whine to it that confuses me while simultaneously piquing my curiosity. The iron clump in my chest shrinks to half its size while I watch the power struggle between the two men play out.

A minute ago, Sawyer's jaw was tight, and his spine was ramrod straight. His eyes held all the authority in the world, just like they did last night. Hell, as they have every other time I've seen him. But now his shoulders hunch slightly, and he frowns like he's giving in. To what, I don't really know.

Angel's stance has been casual this whole time, but his vacant eyes remain unchanged.

He somehow manages to take even longer than Sawyer did to speak, but finally, "Yes, last night I was bluffing."

Sawyer sighs, looking twenty pounds lighter.

"Last night wasn't Ivy's fault," Angel goes on. "I brought her here. I had her call Gaumond. It was my doing."

Sawyer shakes his head. "It's not just that."

"I know. She's a pain in the ass, I agree with you. But she's asking you for another chance. Surely, there's something she can do to make this right?"

When both men look at me at the same time, I drop my gaze to the table and trace the swirling pattern in the wood with my eyes. The iron clump grows.

"She's a manor whore," Sawyer says, the steel back in his voice. He speaks to Angel, but I can feel his gaze on me. "I want to see her act like it."

Act like it.

My heartbeat quickens, and my ears heat.

"Ivy, come here," Angel commands.

I jump at his tone, and my chair scrapes the kitchen tile. I take a deep breath and slowly stand, keeping my eyes down. My instincts tell me to run, but my instincts have already gotten me into a hell of a lot of trouble.

I walk to Angel but don't look up at him, too afraid to see eyes that match that commanding tone. I don't know what it is about it that can make me crumble so easily. I'm not necessarily afraid of him. Or, maybe I am. I don't know, it's hard to tell sometimes by the way my emotions jumble when he's near.

"Get on your knees."

I bite my lip and inhale a sharp breath through my nose, staring straight ahead and consequently giving myself a great view of Angel's chest. He's in nothing but a pair of sweatpants, and if he hadn't immediately terrified me by telling me Sawyer was here when he opened the guest room door this morning, I probably would've had a better chance to admire the carved muscle. This is the most of his skin I've seen, and if this were the end of a date, I'd jump him.

But this isn't the end of a date. This is something totally different.

"Ivy?" Angel prompts.

I lift my eyes to his face, expecting kindness or compassion or something in his expression to match the softness in his voice, but it isn't there. His face is blank, but his eyes are blazing.

"Sawyer would like you to act like a manor whore. Considering how long you've been here and the headache you've caused him, that doesn't seem like such an unreasonable request, does it?"

"No," I say in a small voice.

He searches my eyes for something, and I try not to look away.

"I don't think so either… Nobody has any intention of holding you down, so you do have options." Angel gestures to Sawyer. "Him, me, or no one. Make a choice."

My eyes dart to Sawyer, and his brows jump toward his hairline like he's surprised I'd consider him an option. I don't. I'm just buying time. Most of the time, I think Angel is by far the better of the two, but other times, I wonder if he has any idea how cruel he can be. He thinks he gives people options, but the only options they have is to do what he wants or suffer. He did it to Sawyer last night, and now he's doing it to me.

I turn back to Angel and lower to my knees before he can say anything else. His gray sweats hang low enough to show off his V, and I come face to face with it. I won't lie, I've done worse than this. My husband's affection always came at a price, and that price often involved my humiliation. Even now he's managing to do it.

At least Angel is handsome. Hell, at least he pretends to be a decent human being.

I lick my bottom lip, more out of habit than anything else, before I wrap my fingers around his waistband, brushing hot flesh.

One hand reaches inside his sweats to grip his shaft while I use the other to drag the material down over his hips.

I rake my eyes over his massive erection and am not even remotely surprised that he's already hard.

My tongue slides over my bottom lip again, and I lean toward him, my mouth opening. I close my eyes as I connect with the head of his dick, kissing it before sliding my tongue over the slit.

Angel tenses, and I peek up as he uncrosses his arms. His eyes are wide with surprise, but he quickly schools his expression. I wonder who he's trying to fool, Sawyer or me.

It's sick, I know, but I get a weird satisfaction at watching his hard composure crack, and I'm now glad he chose this. He could've fucked me, but I like this better. I want to make that stupid fucking composure break.

I close my eyes and take more of him into my mouth. My tongue runs along the underside of his shaft, searching until I find a sensitive piece of flesh that has his hips twitching.

I squeeze the base of his dick and lift my other hand to

cup his balls, massaging them gently while I continue to stroke him with my tongue.

Angel clears his throat, and his palm slams on the counter. My lips spread wider as I smile around his girth, taking in more of him until he rams into the back of my throat, and I gag.

"Fuck," Angel hisses. It's in response to pleasure, but in another context, I'd think he was angry.

Sawyer chuckles. "That good, huh?"

Angel ignores Sawyer, and I try to do the same. I can feel him watching me, and if I was a cat who had a life to spare, I'd turn and give him the finger.

I bob my head, gliding over Angel's rigid length, only pausing every now and then to tease that sensitive bundle. I'll give it to him, he's putting up a good front, trying to make it seem like this is truly just a demonstration for Sawyer with the way he stands stock still and tries to remain expression-less. But ultimately, as expected, he breaks.

His hands thread through my hair to grip either side of my head. He stills my movements before starting up again, moving me at his pace and thrusting his hips to fuck my mouth. I'm sure it feels great for him, but I also think it's a man's way of taking back control. And fuck that.

I lightly squeeze his balls while moaning around him, and his rhythm falters. He groans and Sawyer chuckles again, but this time it's stilted, filled with more confusion than with humor.

Angel's hold on me tightens as he bucks his hips with more force. I gag, this time unintentionally, and I massage his balls a little more firmly than before.

His hips still, and his balls tighten. I continue sucking as his salty seed fills my mouth.

I clamp my eyes shut and mewl as if his cum is the most

decadent thing I've ever tasted, keeping at it until he cups my chin and guides me away from him.

He grips the waistband of his sweats and pulls them back up over his hips.

A slow clap sounds behind me, and I force myself not to turn and glower at Sawyer.

"Well fucking done, Ivy," Sawyer chortles, his cruel humor back in full force. "I'm sorry I doubted you."

I keep my head down, purposefully not meeting either man's eyes. I wipe my mouth with the back of my hand and stand, turning away from them. My feet itch to stomp away, but I fight the impulse.

"Can I go to the bathroom?" I ask Angel, my voice not nearly as angry as I expect. It sounds a little more … I don't know, pathetic, than I mean for it to.

"Of course," he says, taking a step toward me and gently brushing his hand over my shoulder. I hurry toward the bathroom before he can touch me anymore and pretend not to hear Sawyer's laughter and crude words at my back.

I close the bathroom door and lock it before spinning to face the mirror. My stomach turns, and I breathe slowly in through my nose in an attempt to keep the nausea at bay.

It doesn't work.

I cover a hand over my mouth and drop to my knees in front of the toilet just as bile rises. Tears blur my vision as I vomit, and I tell myself it's only a physical reaction. But it's a lie. A mountain of shame collapses on top of me, and I brace myself on the toilet bowl long after the semen-bile cocktail empties from my stomach.

What did I just do?

ANGEL

"Satisfied?" I ask Sawyer who's staring at me with the biggest smirk I've ever seen.

He chuckles. "Don't act like you aren't."

I glance toward where Lib just vanished from and feel a twinge of guilt toppling onto the mountain of confusion that's taken up residence in my mind.

I was not expecting that. Not even a little. Honestly, I thought she'd fight it, or at most, give a tentative, ten second blowjob.

That was… Jesus Christ, that was incredible.

I move my gaze back to Sawyer. "You should go."

"And miss my turn?"

My head tilts, and my brows pinch. I pin him with a glare, and he laughs yet again.

"I'm kidding… Kind of. Bring her back to the manor whenever you're ready." He backpedals a step toward the door, waggling his brows. "Never thought I'd say this, but I'm looking forward to having her back."

"Mm-hmm."

He gives me one last grin before spinning and leaving

through the back door. I scratch at the stubble on my cheek and head for the bathroom.

My steps slow when I get near the bathroom door, deflating at the soft cry that filters into the hall. My shoulders hunch and my mouth sinks into a frown.

I sigh and step up to the door, lifting my fist. I knock softly and turn my head so my ear is nearly pressed against the door.

"Ivy?"

Seconds go by without a response, and I sigh. "Are you okay?"

"Fuck off, *Mr. A*," she sneers, emphasizing my title in a way that's more insulting than the, "fuck off."

I glance behind me down the hall and debate over leaving to give her some space. Something tells me that would make things worse.

I turn back toward the door, more guilt sifting in.

"Come on, it wasn't that bad." *It didn't seem like you minded it.* Because I'm not entirely stupid, I don't add that last part.

I grasp the knob and jiggle it, but of course, the door's locked.

I knock again. "Open up so we can talk."

I listen, fully expecting another phrase containing the word 'fuck,' but there's only silence.

Her island name sits on the edge of my tongue, but when I open my mouth, I hesitate. A gust of air rushes past my lips instead. "Lib, *please*."

Another minute passes before the lock clicks and the door opens. Her hand stays on the edge of the door, ready to swing it shut at any moment. Her eyes are glossy and red from crying, but she's wiped the tears from her face.

"Please leave me alone," she says, her voice deceptively even.

"No."

Her lips pucker like she wasn't expecting that. "Why? Are you not done humiliating me?"

"How did I humiliate you?"

Her jaw drops, and her eyes expand in disbelief.

My guilt eases to make room for annoyance. "Last night you broke into my home and threatened to kill me with my own gun, but what, I can't have a fucking blowjob?"

Red tints her cheeks as she closes her mouth.

"I'm not your Prince Charming."

"I never asked you to be." Her voice is soft enough that I bite back my next retort.

Her bloodshot eyes meet mine. "I get what Sawyer was wanting. It was only a matter of time." Her chest rises as she draws in a slow breath. "But did you have to be so eager?"

I scoff. "Did *you*?"

Too far. I can tell by the way she flinches at my words like they physically struck her.

"I'm sorry," I say after a few seconds of silence. "I shouldn't have said that." Another moment passes. "And you're right, I didn't have to be so eager. I'm not sure how to hide the fact that I want you, though, and I don't understand why you would expect me to. I've been pretty up front about my attraction toward you."

She nods, but it seems more out of resignation than agreement. "Fine."

More silence. I'm surprised she hasn't slammed the door in my face.

"You don't have to feel humiliated," I say as gently as I can. "Sawyer doesn't give a shit."

She laughs dryly. "He thought it was hilarious."

Yeah, he did.

"He thought my *reaction* to you was amusing. Neither of us expected you to be a porn star."

Another poor choice of words. Her flinch is even more

pronounced this time, and she points her gaze at the carpet. As an awkward tension forms between us, I finally start to pick up on what's really wrong. She's not horrified by the idea of sucking dick, she's just embarrassed. But why? Because she was good at it?

That doesn't make sense to me.

Regardless, she's hurt. I can see it all over her face.

Guilt churns my stomach.

"I'm sorry." I reach out and trail my fingertips down her arm. "I don't want to hurt you."

"You're not my Prince Charming, remember? Don't backtrack now."

I look up at the ceiling, exhaling through my nose. "I didn't mean that to say I don't care about you. I do. I'm just getting a little tired of having to rescue you while getting nothing in return."

"Like sex?"

"No, like *you*."

Her eyes lift to meet mine as her brow furrows.

"I'm not asking you to fuck me. I just want your trust. I'm not trying to ruin your life here, and I want you to stop treating me as if everything I do is intended to be some affront to you."

A tear leaks from her eye, and she quickly swipes it away.

I step up closer to her and put my hands on her arms. "If it wasn't me today, it would've been Sawyer. You had to give him *something*, Lib."

"Liberty," she whispers, swatting another tear away. "And I know."

"Liberty," I parrot, although I know for certain she goes by Lib. I'm sure it's a 'my friends call me Lib' thing.

Does that bother me? A little. But I get it.

"What an ironic name," I tease in an attempt to lighten the mood.

"Not as ironic as yours."

I laugh at that and caress her face, tipping her chin so she looks at me. Weight lifts from me when I spot a tiny smile that glows with amusement. My lips twitch in return.

"Are you okay?" I ask again, studying her features.

She rubs beneath her eyes, getting rid of the residual tears. "Sure, until I see Sawyer again." She chuckles, but there's little humor to it.

"I'll tell him not to tease so much."

"I'm sure that'll do loads of good."

I finger a lock of her hair and let the sarcasm go. She's probably right. Sawyer can be … insensitive is a nice way of putting it.

I inhale deeply, breathing in her flowery scent. My cock stirs, and my skin heats. Already, I want her again. Being this close… It fucking does something to me.

"Let me make this up to you," I say, my voice heady.

She sways, leaning into my touch, yet it still feels as though she's distancing herself from me at the same time.

"How?"

I flash her a grin and take her hand. "Come with me."

When I turn and tug her hand, she stays put. "Angel…"

I look behind me, watching Lib's throat maneuver as she swallows.

"I mean, Mr. A."

"Yes?"

"What are we doing?"

I squeeze her hand but don't attempt to pull again. "This is what I mean by wanting you to trust me."

Her eyes draw together as she stares at me skeptically. I really can't blame her for this, but I still resent it. Just last night, I told her I killed a woman. My slave, no less.

I should be patient, understanding, kind.

But I'm not. Because to me, this is a woman I've been

vying for for years. I've already spent a huge amount of time invested in her. To her, I'm just a guy she met once years ago and has known for a couple of weeks. I'm someone to use, not someone to trust.

So yeah, it bothers me.

After a minute, her face softens, and I watch the resolve cross her expression. I try to guide her again, and this time she lets me. I lead her upstairs and into my bedroom. We lock eyes, but when I shut the door a moment later, she quickly looks away.

I take her hand again and urge her to the bed, amazed when she doesn't protest.

"Lay down," I say, gently prodding her.

"Under the covers?"

"No."

She bites her lip and stands tall and tense for several seconds, her arms stiff by her sides. After several long beats of silence, she hesitantly climbs on the bed and lays down on her back, her gaze finding me. She studies me, searching for some sinister intention. I'm trying to keep my face impassive, but I don't know that there's any hiding the erection I have growing inside my pants. Her eyes find it, and my cock jumps. I ignore it the best I can and sit on the bed.

This isn't about me. Not this time.

I run my hands from her shins to her knees, and when I try to pry them apart, she doesn't budge. I lift my eyes to meet hers.

"What are you doing?" she asks.

"Trust me."

She stares at me, clearly unsure. The T-shirt I laid at the end of her bed while she slept stops mid-thigh, and I have to force myself not to pull it up.

With great reluctance, she relaxes her knees. I open her legs and climb on the bed to situate myself between them. A hiss slips past her lips when I lift the T-shirt up and tuck my fingers under the waistband of her panties. She stiffens, and when I drag her panties down over her hips, she inhales sharply.

So do I. But for a very different reason.

I spread her legs wider to get a better look at her pink pussy, and my mouth waters. I stop trying to keep my expression neutral and let the desire taking over me show. It doesn't matter anyway... Lib's face is turned so she isn't looking at me.

"Do you trust me?" I ask.

I think for sure she'll say no, but she surprises me by nodding. I'm not convinced, but I like the lie.

My hands smooth up her thighs before I run two fingers up her surprisingly slick folds. Lib's hands form tight balls clutching the comforter, mimicking the tension in her crinkled eyelids. A shiver runs down my spine, and I lick my lips.

She gasps when I press my thumb against her clit, gently rubbing up and down.

"Relax," I coo. "You're not the only one who knows how to give oral."

"All men think they're good at oral," she says with nervous amusement. "I hate to break it to you, but women are far better at faking than men are at doing."

I chuckle. "Oh yeah? Did you fake your orgasms with Robert?"

Her expression buckles, and a sadness overtakes her face. Fuck, I am terrible with words.

I don't need her to answer anyway. I already know.

"Do me a favor," I say to pull Lib's mind away from wherever she just went. I shift onto my stomach, resting my head against her inner thigh. "Don't fake it."

Before she can respond, I slide my tongue from her taint

to her clit, and her thighs clamp around me. I tuck my hands underneath her legs to pull them apart.

My eyes close as I run my tongue up and down, tasting her. This part is mostly for me, although by the way she squirms, her back arching, I'd say she likes it. One taste, and I'm already an addict.

I force my hand around her thigh, spreading her wider, and use my thumb to rub circles on her clit. My tongue finds her honey-filled hole, and I slide inside, nuzzling my face against her while she subtly tries to pull away. I don't think it's her body fighting it, though, I'm pretty certain it's her mind.

I fuck her with my tongue while increasing pressure on her clit, earning me a delicious moan. Another follows, and my cock strains painfully, blue balls already beginning to set in. Her moans almost sound reluctant, like she's doing her best to hold back. Like she doesn't want to believe I can unravel her as efficiently as she can unravel me.

Game on.

I drag my tongue up to her clit and purse my lips around it before sucking. Lib lets out a loud whimper while her hands thread into my hair and tug.

I fit a finger inside her and massage her walls, focusing my angle upward and searching until a low mewl signals I've found her G-spot.

I lick her clit, my tongue flat and firm, while sliding my finger back and forth inside her, increasing the pressure each time I hit the spot that has her pulling my hair.

"Fuck," she groans, her legs gripping my head and forcing me closer. I guess her mind gave up.

Something slaps the headboard, and I open my eyes to see her knuckles turning white as she grips the bottom of it like she's hanging on for dear life.

Her hips gyrate, meeting each of my thrusts. I insert

another finger, relishing in the way her face contorts with pleasure. When she arches her back to lift herself higher, I shove my free hand under her ass to hold her up.

She rocks back and forth against my face, showing me the speed that she likes, teaching me something about Lib that I should've already known. She likes control. Unfortunately for her, so do I.

I remind myself this is for her and let her guide my movements. An idea strikes.

I pull away from Lib, and her eyes shoot open. She lets go of the headboard and braces herself on her elbows to look at me, her eyes holding a plea that has me burning with desire.

"Get up," I order, unwrapping her legs from me.

A frown bows her lips as she pulls herself to a sitting position, but her eyes shine with interest when I shift up the bed and lay down on my back. I grab her hips and pull her toward me, and she understands what I want without me having to spell it out for her.

She throws her leg over me and positions herself to straddle my face. She lowers her pussy to my mouth, her T-shirt draping over me as I press my tongue inside her.

My fingers dig into her ass while I lick from her hole to her clit and back. When her hips start to move, I position my tongue on her clit and let her grind against me.

My vision is swallowed up by the T-shirt, so I have to settle on hearing alone to enjoy her loud moan and her palms slamming onto the top of the headboard. I suck her clit harder while she essentially fucks my face, and when her muscles seize, I quickly move to her hole to taste her when she comes.

Her thighs muffle her scream of approval for me, but it's no less satisfying. As she comes down from her orgasm, her legs shake and her heavy breathing plays a symphony for my ears.

She slowly pulls a trembling leg over me before collapsing onto the bed. She shifts next me, and I drag her to lay on my chest. My fingers lazily glide over her shoulder as I stare up at the ceiling through hooded eyelids.

Lib slides her leg on top of mine and nuzzles her knee against my erection.

I let out a breathless laugh. "That's not fair."

"What, you don't like to be teased?"

"No." I look down at her and smile. She smiles back, but then lets it slowly fall.

"What?" I ask, fingering a lock of her hair.

Her eyes glisten in post-orgasm bliss, but there's something else there too.

"Do you really want me to call you Mr. A?"

I consider her question for half a second before shaking my head. "Not when we're alone, no." I run my fingers through her hair. "But I'd prefer it if you called me Mr. A when anyone else is around. Sawyer has a thing about names, with the manor whores, at least… It's a power thing."

She nods absently and looks away. "Okay."

"Hey." I caress her face, then tilt it so she's looking at me. "If it's a problem for you, we'll break that particular rule. Fuck Sawyer."

She shakes her head. "It's not that."

"Then what is it?"

She lets out a soft breath. "I fucking hate being called Ivy."

I give her a small, understanding smile. "Then I won't call you Ivy."

"Like, at all?"

"Like, at all."

"You won't care if Sawyer gets pissed?"

I shake my head.

"But what if he—"

"Liberty."

She closes her mouth, and I run my thumb over her lips. "You're safe with me. I promise."

For the first time since I met her, she looks like she believes me. She snuggles her head against my chest and closes her eyes, her arm stretching across my abs to hug me close.

"Angel?"

"Hmm?"

She sighs, her breath kissing my skin.

"Thank you."

19

LIBERTY

My hips sway to music that reminds me of my days in college.

I'd be out at a club with friends, usually my roommates, Tori and Mia. We'd start out sticking together, allowing the occasional guy to cut into our space if we deemed him worthy. At some point in the night, when our vision blurred and our heads were light enough for us to drift away in the arms of a barely-man in his early twenties, we'd break up.

We had an agreement that we would always find each other before leaving the club with someone, and every hour we'd meet in the bathroom to check in. We thought we were so clever about the careful way we stuck together, not capable of even imagining just how dark the world was back then. There's this illusion of invincibility when you're young that no amount of CNN or stories of adolescent death can take away.

Date rape happened to girls who left their drinks unattended when they went to the bathroom. The ones who got too smashed at parties or the ones who didn't have a check-in system with their friends when they went on dates. Not us. We were far too smart.

I laugh out loud at my clueless, younger self, my hips still swaying, prying eyes still pinned on me through the bars of the cage. They can't hear my laughter over the music, but if they could, I wonder if they'd think I'd gone insane.

When the song stops, I grip the pole with both hands and slide down, pausing until a new song comes on. A fast beat sounds through the speakers in the playroom, and I slide back up, my exposed breasts grazing the warm metal.

I'm in nothing but a thong that could double as floss, so when I flip myself around, my back pressing against the pole, I give the man standing with his hands flat against the stage a front row seat to my naked body.

I trail my hands up my hips, over my navel to my tits, then I lean my head back, lips parted as if I'm enjoying this. I think some of them, some as oblivious as Angel, believe the act. There are women on this island who want to be here. I've met them. I've listened to them. I've tried, and failed, to understand them. Regardless of whether I get it or not, they exist.

Even more surprising than that, there are men here who don't possess dark desires that would make someone want to hide underneath a bed. They're here because they like the kink. They like the women who like the kink. They have loads of money to pay for it, and they're accustomed to doing whatever the fuck they want.

They remind me so much of the spoiled, rich boys at Harvard, the ones I subtly grinded on in the club, except now they're grown men who don't need to buy a drink first before their entitlement sets in. Now all they have to pay is a fee to live on this island.

But then there's the other category of men—one in which my biggest fan with his hand on the stage belongs to—who are here because modern society won't let them hurt women the way this island allows. Their resident fee is a ticket for a time machine back to the caveman era. They're the ones with the sick needs Sawyer referred to the first time we met. They're the ones who come to the playroom solely to hunt, not to play. I'm also pretty sure they're the entire reason people like me are forced onto the island. They're not interested in consent, they're interested in maximum pain, and the kidnapped women are the ones who provide it for them.

Sawyer won't admit to any of this, and none of the other women have confirmed my theory, but I can't help but notice the manor whores are the ones who came here willingly and are happy to be in the playroom. The forced ones seem to be sold within weeks of being brought here.

Coincidence? I doubt it.

My thoughts drift to Naomi, and I close my eyes, shutting down the worry before it has a chance to consume me. She hasn't been here for the last week, and no one can tell me anything about what's happened to her. Sawyer and I don't speak, and Angel has been away on business, so I haven't been able to ask him.

He's back tonight, though. He should already be at his house, waiting up for me like he said he would. I only have another hour, and then I can leave here and get my answers. So for now, I ignore the questions.

My eyes fly open when someone grabs my ankle, and I make the mistake of looking down, finding my admirer. I learned after the first few days of dancing on this stage that it's best not to make eye contact with anyone. That's when you see the menacing lust in people's gazes.

And it's there now, pooling in the man's dark eyes. He's been here every night this week, always staring up at me, daring me to look closer at the evil in his smile so his intentions can be made crystal clear.

He isn't here to play. He's here to hunt. He's one of those guys.

My heart gallops, and my body goes rigid. My skin freezes where he touches me, but I don't pull away nor do I look at his hand. I stare into his eyes, doing my best not to give him the fear I know he's after.

Someone boos and another person joins in. The Instant the man lets go of my ankle, I turn around, searching the crowd for Angel in hope that he decided to come. Unsurprisingly, I don't see him, but I do lock eyes with Sawyer across the room.

He's with another man who's leaned toward him, speaking over the music. For a few moments—until the boos become too loud to ignore—I'm pinned by Sawyer's stare. I blink, bringing my attention back to the audience as I start swaying again, keeping my gaze away from my unwanted admirer.

A half hour passes before I no longer feel the guy's eyes, and I catch his back as he walks away. I let out a sigh of relief and finish my last half hour feeling more comfort than I would've thought possible.

After I leave the playroom, I head back to my shared bedroom to throw on a pair of mesh shorts and a gray, V-neck shirt. I slip on a pair of flip-flops and head out of the room and down a hall, making the trek to the back door.

Because I'm not allowed to have the gate's passcode—shocker—I have to find a guard to escort me to Angel's house. Specifically, I need to find Cooper, one of the extra guards Sawyer hired after my escape attempt, since he's supposed to be the one stationed at the back of the manor tonight.

My shoes slap the tile, and I feel more and more at ease with each step. I'm not saying Angel and I are best buds, but I can admit that life is a hell of a lot better when he's here. For one, I don't have to work as much. For two, the guards are nicer when the threat of Angel's presence exists. And for three, honestly, it's just nice to have someone I can really talk to without risk of punishment. Someone who's allowed to say my name.

The back door is in my sight when my admirer appears, and the slapping of my shoes ceases. My eyes widen, but I quickly right myself, knowing my surprise and fear are what he's after.

"Hi," he says, his face lighting up with a smile filled with everything but kindness. "How are you?"

I detect a slight accent and squint as if that'll help me decipher it. I'd guessed all this time that he was American.

"Great," I say sarcastically. "I'm on my way to see someone, so if you'll excuse me…"

I force my limbs to move in his direction, holding my breath as I near him. He grabs my arm to stop me and chuckles as he whips me back around, causing me to stumble.

"Wow, for a manor whore, you're awfully cold. Aren't you supposed to be more inviting?"

British. He's British.

"No." My tone is deadpan, and I hope my expression matches it. "Now let me the fuck go."

His eyes widen with surprise, but he corrects the expression as quickly as I did, his face relaxing. "Feisty one, aren't you?" He laughs salaciously as he runs his hand up my arm. "I like that."

"Yeah, you'll like it even more when my thumbs are in your eye sockets. Let me the fuck go. *Now.*"

His grip on me tightens to the point of pain, and I bite my tongue to keep from yelping.

He leans in close, nuzzling his nose in my hair before inhaling. His own smell, a foresty cologne, floods my senses, and although it might be pleasant on another man, my nose crinkles with disgust.

"The person I'm supposed to be meeting is very powerful and very impatient," I say as I wrench my arm from his grasp. "I'm already late, and I promise, if I tell him you're what held me up, he'll be pissed."

"Oh, really?" he pulls back, wearing a simpering smile. "And how will he know how to find me? You don't even know my name, sweetheart."

I keep my face stoic, but I can clearly see his point. I was bluffing anyway. Considering Angel is cool with me dancing naked in a cage for an audience of horny men, I'm guessing he wouldn't be too concerned about one of them stopping to talk to me.

"Here, I'll help." His dark eyes shift to my breasts, and I feel equally exposed as I did when I was shirtless. "My name is Jasper Flynn. You can tell your friend I made you late if it keeps you out of trouble."

His leer intensifies when he sees me affected by my failed attempt to intimidate him. "And you're right. Angel is an impatient asshole."

He knows Angel?

He knew he's who I was going to see?

How?

"Tell him I say hello." Jasper winks. I expect him to leave, but he continues to tower over me, just an inch away.

I blink a few times then hurry around him toward the back door.

"See you tomorrow, Ivy," he calls to my back. I cringe but keep walking. I don't turn back, and even though I know he isn't following, I feel his presence like a ghost that's clinging to me.

I find Cooper hanging around outside, probably waiting for me, and he escorts me to Angel's house without either of us saying a word. Sometimes, I can't tell if Cooper is so reserved because of his personality, or if Angel just scares him speechless.

I walk through the back door and eagerly dart my eyes around for Angel. "Hello?" No response. "Angel?"

I walk into the living room and hear a faint voice coming from the hallway. I follow the voice, stopping when I reach the door that's been locked every other time I've been here.

Angel's voice is louder now, and I recognize his tone from when he's irritated. I glance down the hall, debating on hanging out in the living room instead of letting him know I'm here, but then I turn back to the door and raise my fist.

I knock lightly, then put my hand on the knob, opening the door slowly before peeking my head inside. Angel's sitting at his desk, a phone pressed to his ear. Not his cell phone this time, an office phone.

He fucking has an office phone. The mental image of smacking myself in the head flows into my mind.

"Hold on a sec," he tells whoever he's on the phone with. He stabs a button and spins in his chair to fully face me.

"Hey, beautiful," he says, a tiny smile tugging his lips.

"Hey."

"Give me a few minutes to finish this up, okay?"

I lift my chin. "Sure." I pull back and close the door before walking toward the living room. My lips sag as I realize how reminiscent that exchange was to past exchanges with Robert. Only Robert would've been pissed at me for opening the door to his office. Judging by the way Angel always keeps his office locked, I'd venture to guess he's just as secretive.

I grab the horror book I've been reading off the shelf in the living room and flop down on the couch before flipping it open. I'm typically a romance reader, but I haven't been in the mood for happy endings—gee, I wonder why—so Stephan King is my go-to guy right now.

I find where I left off and try to concentrate on the words, but I can't get Jasper Flynn's depraved eyes out of my mind. Or the fact that he knew I was going to see Angel.

Just how much does he know about me?

I blink away my thoughts when Angel's office door opens and shuts. I turn my head to look at him just as he appears.

"Sorry about that," he says, walking up to the couch.

I stick the bookmark back inside *Pet Cemetery* and set the book on the end table. "Who were you talking to?"

"Conference call. Don't worry about it."

Yup, he's secretive.

I narrow my eyes. "At one in the morning?"

"It's nine P.M. in China. Emergency thing… Like I said, don't worry about it."

"Are you going to have to leave again?" My heart picks up speed as I stare at Angel while he takes his time answering me.

He sits on the couch next to me and rests his arm behind me. "I missed you." He brushes his knuckles over my shoulder.

"Are you going to have to leave again?" I repeat, letting my annoyance show.

He sighs and pulls his hand away, running it through his hair and closing his eyes. Eventually, he nods, and my heart drops into my stomach.

I turn to face forward and stare at the shelf my book will go when I leave here. At this rate, it should only take me six years to finish it.

"You know, I find it strange how you get pissed when I leave, yet you don't seem to be happy when I'm here."

I turn to face him, ready to fight, but the disappointment on his face stops me. I'm disappointed too. We just show it differently.

I stare at him a few moments, feeling my vulnerability as

it bubbles to the surface. I try to live in the moment, to feel the safety I currently have with Angel sitting beside me, but I can't see past Jasper Flynn. I can't get him telling me he'll see me tomorrow out of my head.

"Jasper Flynn says hi," I say when I can't think of another way to respond to him. I don't think he could possibly understand the truth if I gave it to him.

I'm not *happy* when he's here. I'm relieved. Really fucking relieved because it means life is a little bit safer for me, and it means for a couple hours a night, when it's just the two of us, I get to be myself. I'm not interested in playing board games and telling stories, I just want to be here and be angry without being punished for it. That's what he provides me. He'd never understand that.

Angel narrows his eyes. "Excuse me?"

"After he was done eye-fucking me in the playroom, he stopped me before I came here. He told me to tell you he says hi."

I watch Angel's face, searching for any hint of jealousy, but all I find is confusion.

"How do you know his name?"

That's what he focuses on? Not the eye-fucking part?

Asshole.

"He told me."

Angel's brow furrows as he moves his gaze to the coffee table.

"Why does it matter?"

"He shouldn't be telling you his name," Angel mutters under his breath. It sounds more like he's talking to himself than to me.

"Why? Who is he?"

Angel's eyes move back to me. "He's a friend of mine. And Sawyer's, *mostly* Sawyer's. We met in college."

I stare at him, waiting for him to go on. He looks like he's finished, but when it's clear I'm not satisfied, he continues.

"He just moved here a few weeks ago. He must not be aware of the rules yet."

I have to force myself not to roll my eyes. "Or he doesn't care about them."

"Maybe." It's the obvious truth. "Either way, stay away from him. He's … dangerous."

"Yeah, I got that impression." I remain impassive even though bugs run beneath my skin at hearing Angel confirm what I already know.

See you tomorrow night, Ivy.

Silence ensues for a minute before Angel gets up and starts toward the kitchen. "Thirsty?"

"Yeah," I say, getting up and following him. "And hungry."

He pulls two glasses from the cabinet as I pass him. I open the fridge while he grabs a bottle from the liquor cabinet.

I had my heart set on a sandwich, but when I spot the box of Godiva chocolates—my favorite guilty pleasure—my eyes lock onto them.

There's a split second of excitement. A split second where I feel the tiniest bit of comfort bleeding in from my old life.

But then a thought occurs to me that leaves nothing but questions in its wake… How could he know?

My lips part, and I don't turn around when I hear Angel pouring the glasses or when I feel him come toward me.

"Decisions, decisions," he says, teasing me for taking so long. He thinks I'm debating on what to choose, but really, I'm just dumbstruck. This must be a coincidence. He doesn't *know* this is my comfort food … right?

Sawyer does.

But I must have told him months ago.

There's no way Angel could remember that, even if Sawyer briefly mentioned it or if Angel read it somehow.

I glance at Angel, then point to the chocolates. "Is it all right if I have one of those?"

He gives me a small smile and nods. "They're for you. I picked them up when I was in The States."

I turn back to the fridge and just stare.

"Is something wrong?"

"No," I reply, my voice too soft. I blink, clear my throat, and grab the box before shutting the fridge. Angel follows me to the kitchen table, glasses in hand, and we take seats next to each other.

Gingerly, I open the box, staring at the selection before choosing a coconut flavored truffle. A memory of Ellie and I last winter pops into my mind, and I close my eyes. Robert was on a trip, and it was just her and me in the house. We ate pizza and watched a scary movie, face clay hardening our cheeks. We did it up like a true slumber party, and I remember how happy I felt then. How happy we both felt. We bought a box of these chocolates and took turns eating with our eyes closed to see who could guess the most correctly.

After Ellie went to bed, I stayed up until three in the morning talking to saltyshells... Sawyer. That was when I told him about the chocolate.

A knot forms in my stomach, and I set the box back down, feeling blood drain from my face.

"What's wrong?" Angel asks, real concern in his voice.

I shake my head, internally cursing the pins pricking my eyes. "Nothing."

"Liberty, come on. What is it?"

I shake my head again, but I'm not trying to fool him now. I close my eyes and rub my lids with my thumbs. When I open my eyes, I take a deep breath and let out something between a groan and a laugh. "Fucking Sawyer," I say, trying to put as much amusement into the words as possible.

Angel's face pinches with concern. "What about him?"

I gesture to the chocolates. "He just… He has to taint every good fucking memory I have."

"What are you talking about?"

I pull my eyes from the box to look at Angel. "Sawyer told you this is my comfort food."

Angel rears back. "What?"

I gesture to the box. "He told you. That's why you brought this back for me."

The lines between his eyes deepen. "Are you serious?"

I open my mouth to go on but then close it. Am I overreacting here?

"Didn't he?" I ask, now the one who's confused.

He gives his head a shake and takes a swig of his drink, a brown liquor. I'm guessing from my time spent with Angel that it's whiskey.

After he sets the glass down, his serious eyes assess me. "I don't know what all you think Sawyer and I talk about, but no, he didn't tell me that."

"Oh." A blush heats my cheeks, and I suddenly feel stupid.

"You don't have to be so worried about him knowing intimate details about you. He talks to three women at a time, on average, so I doubt he remembers much about you other than the big things."

"But…"

"But what?"

I clear my throat again. "You knew my favorite drink. You said you read transcripts."

Angel tilts his head. "What's your favorite drink?"

"A Manhattan."

He chuckles. "Liberty, you're *from* Manhattan. I didn't know that was your favorite drink, it was just what popped into my mind in that moment. You're talking about that night in the playroom, right?"

I bob my head.

"When I said I'd read transcripts, I just meant I read a little. I know big things about you, important things. I know you went to Harvard, you dropped out of law school four years ago when you married Robert, and you have parents in Florida who you talk to twice a year. That's pretty much the extent of it."

I'm quiet for a minute, considering what he's telling me.

So the drink was a coincidence. The chocolate is a coincidence.

Of course it is. Of course it doesn't make sense for Sawyer to tell Angel all of that, or for either man to even care about those things. Angel's right, Sawyer probably doesn't even remember any of that shit.

But when I spoke to him, when I opened up my heart and poured myself into him like a floodgate bursting, it felt so real. It felt like he knew me. It felt like he maybe even *loved* me.

Jesus, I'm delusional. I've got to stop separating the Sawyer I thought I knew with the Sawyer who exists.

It was all an illusion. A lie.

He doesn't even care.

"Oh," I say at last, forcing a tiny smile. "Well, good. I guess I was overreacting."

"It makes sense to be confused," he says, though I doubt he means it. "Sawyer's very good at making people feel like he cares... He's practiced at it."

Angel reaches across the table and puts his hand over mine, smiling sadly. "Don't let it taint the good memories, okay?"

I hum, knowing he's right.

"I'm sorry for upsetting you."

"No." I pull the box of chocolates toward me and look at Angel. "This was kind. *Thank you.*"

He gives my forearm a quick squeeze. "You're welcome."

I pick at the coconut truffle again. When I taste the first bite, I close my eyes and try not to cry as memories assail me. I want to remember. I want to appreciate my life and all the joy it's brought me. So why does it make me so fucking sad?

"I'll be able to stay for a few days," Angel says, eliciting me to open my eyes. "Then I have to go to Shanghai, but I won't be gone long."

I swallow, leaving a coconut aftertaste in my mouth. "How long?"

"It depends." He hikes up a shoulder. "Two days. Four tops."

I nod slowly, trying to accept it.

See you tomorrow night, Ivy.

"I'm here now, though." He puts his hand on mine and squeezes. "I'll tell Sawyer you won't be working the next couple of nights. Would you like that?"

I pick at another truffle. "Yes. Thank you," I say, my voice soft.

"You're welcome... Let's talk about something else, okay? I'm pissed I have to go, and I don't want to dwell on it while you're here."

"Okay," I agree.

He smiles and picks up his drink, emptying the glass when he knocks it back. I follow suit and let the whiskey burn my throat.

"What would you like to do?" he asks.

I already know. I've been thinking about it all day.

I set the glass down with a grimace, coughing into my shoulder. Clearing my throat, I meet Angel's gaze. "Do you think we could watch the news?"

Something passes over his face, and immediately, I know he doesn't want to. Or rather, he doesn't want me to. I'm sure it's another one of Sawyer's rules.

I press on anyway. "What could it possibly hurt?"

He lets out a long breath. "How about a movie instead?"

I'm quiet for a moment, a little disappointed but also a little excited. I'm a big movie buff.

"Anything you want," he adds with an encouraging tilt of his lips.

I bite my lip while I think about it. My eyes travel to the living room where my book is. If I won't be able finish the book, I may as well watch the movie.

I turn back to Angel. "Pet Cemetery."

He tips his head to the side. "Really?"

"What? Pegged me as a chick flick kind of girl?"

"Actually, yeah."

"That's because I am one." I give him a mischievous smile and stand from the table. "Let's go watch some people with shittier lives than me."

His shoulders shake with a chuckle as he stands. I grab the box of chocolates before we head to the living room.

An hour and a half later, my head is rested on his thigh, my knees pulled into my chest. I stare at the screen, watching horrors that make me question the writer's sanity, but I'm not really seeing anything. I haven't been paying attention to most of the movie, which I guess means I'll have to finish the book after all.

Angel shifts, and I close my eyes, my cheek warm against his slacks. His arm rests on my back as he caresses my shoulders, sending tingles down my limbs with each touch.

I like this. I fight it, so hard. I tell myself that I should hate Angel, but I can't. He's the only good thing on this island. Him and Naomi.

Naomi.

My eyes snap open, and a rush of guilt flows into me for being so consumed with my own life that I forgot about hers.

"Where's Naomi?" I ask, sitting up abruptly.

Angel startles at my sudden urgency before grabbing the remote to pause the movie. "What?"

"Naomi, my... You know, April? Do you know where she is?"

Angel shakes his head, his eyes sleepy. "No..."

"But you can find out, right?"

He's quiet for a few moments.

"Angel?"

"Yes, Liberty, I'll find out."

"Could you do it now?"

Angel's head tilts as he stares at me, taking his time to respond. "Why is this suddenly a pressing matter?"

Because I'm a shitty, shitty *friend.*

"I... It just is."

He nods slowly, like he's reading my mind. "I can't find out anything tonight, but I will tomorrow."

"But why? Can't you just text Sawyer and—"

"No." He says it with a finality that has my lips pressing together. After a moment, he sighs. "If Sawyer is at the manor, he doesn't have his cell phone. If he's home, he doesn't want to be bothered. It's the middle of the night."

I deflate, diverting my eyes as my body slumps.

Angel cups my face and guides me to look at him. "Don't do that."

"Do what?"

"Don't look so *defeated.* You're stronger than that."

I drop my gaze, avoiding his eyes this time when he caresses my jaw.

He sighs. "I promise, wherever Naomi is won't change just because I ask. It makes no difference whether you find out tonight or tomorrow."

I remain quiet, still not able to meet his eyes. I know he's right, and it's worse than that. It won't make a difference what he finds out tomorrow or the next day or whenever he decides to ask for me. He isn't going to change her situation. He won't even change mine.

"Liberty…" He pushes my hair off my face before taking my chin and forcing me to look at him. "We were good just a minute ago. What happened?"

"If something's happened to her and she needs help … are you going to help her?"

His eyelashes flicker, confirming what I already know. I don't need him to answer verbally.

After an impossible amount of time, he takes my cheek and roams his gaze over my face. "Is it not enough for me to protect you?"

I scoff and pull away. Frustration draws his lips into a thin line, and he doesn't reach out to me again.

"You're not protecting me. You *can't* protect me. You're not even here."

His eyes narrow, but he doesn't respond.

"Tonight, men watched me dance naked in a fucking cage, Angel, and you don't even care."

"You have to give Sawyer something. No one is expecting you to fuck anyone, but you have to contribute somehow, and this is the best option."

"Why?" I ask, frustrated tears pricking my eyes. "Why do I *have* to give Sawyer anything? He already took my fucking freedom."

Angel's face softens as he releases a long breath through his nose. "I know."

I take Angel's hands, scooting as close to him as possible. It seems like I'm always desperate when I'm around him. Begging, pleading… Pathetic.

"I'm not safe like this. No one at the manor is. You have to know that."

Angel looks away.

"If I was yours…"

"*Stop*, Liberty."

"It would be almost the *exact* same thing. You're gone so much, all it would be is me hanging out in your house."

He barks out a laugh. "Yeah, that sounds like an excellent idea."

My brain races. "Then I could stay at the manor while you're away. Isn't that what other women do while their..." I struggle to say the word, like acid on my tongue, "master ... leaves the island?"

"I don't care what other people do. I do not own slaves. Period."

My mouth opens and closes while my brain searches for words that could appeal to him. That could make him change his mind. This isn't the first time I've hinted at this—him never acknowledging the attempts—but it's the first time I've asked him outright.

"*Please*," I beg when I can't think of anything else. "I can't do this forever."

His lips separate, and I can see the venom he's about to spew. That's how it works with us. I say shit I shouldn't, and he says shit to shut me up. It's a never-ending battle between us. He must see the pitiful plea in my expression because he stops himself, his eyes softening and mouth closing.

I climb on top of him, straddling his thighs, and put my hands on either side of his face. "*Please*." His face twists with pain, and I press my lips to his before he can give me an answer that'll hurt me.

His lips relax, and when my tongue darts out, he opens his mouth for me. Even my kiss is desperate, too hard, too hurried.

He urges my shoulders back, breaking away from me. His voice is soft when he speaks, like he's afraid I'll fracture. "That's enough."

"It wouldn't be the same as before. It doesn't have to—"

"Enough." He shoves me off him, and I land on my elbows on the couch, my legs still slung over his lap. I slowly pull my legs away, expecting a river of tears to come, but they don't. I don't feel sad. I feel hopeless.

I plant my feet on the floor and face the TV, staring at a stilled image of a dead cat.

"I'm sorry," Angel says, sounding pained. "I just..."

"You can't," I finish for him.

Silence engulfs the room as we sit awkwardly within inches of one another, no idea who should speak first. Unsure how we'll be able to move on from this.

It's simple for me... I need him. I really fucking need him, no matter how much I hate it.

He doesn't need me.

"I'm sorry," I finally say. My heart rate picks up thinking about the possibility of him changing his mind about me. He could throw me away, just like that. He holds so much power over me, and I never seem to remember it until I give him a reason to exert it. "I shouldn't have pressed."

More silence.

"Please don't tell me to leave," I say, closing my eyes, barely holding myself together. "I won't bring it up again."

Angel sighs and scoots closer to me. He runs the back of his fingers down my arm then back up again, across my spine, down the other arm. He leans in and plants a kiss to the shell of my ear. He pushes the hair off my shoulder, brushes my neck with his lips, lowers himself to my collarbone, each kiss pulling more fear from me than the last.

It's okay, he tells me without saying the words. *It's going to be okay.*

I wish I could believe him.

See you tomorrow night, Ivy.

I shudder at the unwanted voice in my head, trying not to think about everything it means.

I lean in to Angel's touch, his hands tugging at the collar of my shirt, his lips kissing my chest. I let him lie to me, let him push the unwanted thoughts from my mind.

He coaxes me to lie down on the couch, his mouth never leaving me. He lifts up my shirt and kisses the well of my breasts, his tongue snaking out, wetting my skin.

He works his lips down my chest, over my stomach to my waist. I arch my hips to help him as he removes my shorts, and I close my eyes at the jolt of sensation that rushes through me when his tongue slides up my slit.

He sucks and licks, opening my legs wider while I relax into the couch, giving in. Minutes pass while he works his magic, my longer breaths turning to pants, my hands gripping his hair.

When I come, I moan his name just because I love the sound of it, love the freedom it gives me.

He pulls away from my sex and drags himself up my body to kiss my mouth, making me taste myself. His kisses are slower this time, less desperate. I moan as his tongue, just seconds after bringing me ecstasy, glides over my lower lip.

I open my mouth for him, letting him kiss me, touch me, all without owning me. I listen to him, obey his unsaid commands, live in the moment with him. And the entire time, I forget I'm a whore.

Angel shifts us so we're lying with his chest pressed to my back on the couch, then he lifts himself up just enough to grab the remote. He turns the movie back on before pulling me closer, both of us pretending we're concentrating on the screen.

"Do you actually hate your life?" Angel eventually asks, sounding like he's afraid to hear the answer. As if he did this to me. A month ago, I blamed him. Now I only blame Sawyer.

I don't need time to consider the question.

"Yes ... but it's better when you're here."

He sighs into my hair, and I close my eyes.

"I'll stay."

My eyes fly open. Did I hear him wrong?

"Sawyer can go on my behalf. It's about time he takes a turn anyway."

He moves his hand from my hip to my stomach, cuddling me close. "That means I'll be in charge of the manor while he's gone… If you *really* don't want to dance, I won't force you."

"If I don't, you'll just make someone else."

He doesn't respond. When his hold on me loosens, I grab his hand and hug it to me before he can pull away.

"I'll dance… Thank you for staying."

He nuzzles into my hair and inhales, similar to how the predator did earlier tonight. Forcing Jasper from my mind, I melt into Angel, and a warmth swims from my chest to my belly. Two men. Same action. Two drastically different responses.

As the credits for the movie play, I watch the words move up the screen. Neither of us reach for the remote to shut off the TV, and when I hear Angel's slow, heavy breaths in my ear, I realize he's asleep.

I close my eyes, listening to the movie's insidious soundtrack play, hoping it's not a sign of what's to come.

2 0

———

LIBERTY

When I arrive at the manor in the morning, four girls are huddled around the pool in the usual gossip spot. When one glimpses me, she shushes the others, and they all stare as I walk by.

By the looks on their faces, I can tell something's off, but I don't bother trying to pry it out of them. I continue inside and head upstairs to my bedroom, intent on taking a shower and changing. But when I notice Desiree and Lily whispering to each other, I pause.

They're standing in front of their room like something's keeping them from going in. I want to ask what's going on, but Desiree and I have come to a silent agreement that we're not going to acknowledge each other's existence.

I don't know what Angel said to her, if anything, after she set me up, but she hasn't thrown me more than a dirty look in the month since I tried to escape.

Lily notices me, and she pokes Desiree on the shoulder and points my way. Desiree turns, and as soon as our eyes meet, a grin spreads across her face. She glances at the door, then back at me, her mischievous smile so wide, it makes her look like The Grinch.

Lily looks more nervous than anything, biting a nail and shifting from foot to foot. Her ponytail sways as she moves her head between Desiree and me.

They begin my way, Desiree taking the lead, and I consider going into my room but don't. I can tell Desiree is about to break our unspoken agreement, and if anyone is going to tell me what's up, it's her. Her version of reality, at least.

"Hey, *Ivy*," Desiree says, her voice sugary sweet. I don't know whose benefit it's for. "Just get back from the crematorium?"

My eyes narrow to slits, but I don't say anything. You don't have to say anything to Desiree in order for her to run her mouth.

I move my focus to Lily who gives me an apologetic smile with plenty of nervousness attached. "Is something going on?"

She opens her mouth, but Desiree cuts in. "You'd know if you weren't whoring yourself out for special treatment."

I flick my eyes to Desiree for the briefest second before turning back to Lily.

"It's April," Lily whispers like she's afraid the walls have ears. In all fairness, they do. "She just got back."

My eyes widen, and I go to step around the women, but Desiree takes my arm. I swing my head her way.

"She's pretty banged up. You should probably let her rest."

Banged up?

My stomach lurches.

"Where was she?" I ask, unable to help it when my voice raises several octaves.

Desiree smirks, and I could fucking kill her.

"She was with a new resident, Mr. J," Lily replies, then turns to look at Desiree. "Isn't that what you said?"

Desiree nods, never taking her eyes off me. "I believe you've met him, Ivy. He's the second man who's asked me where you were since you've been here."

I nearly double over as Jasper's face comes into my mind, and I see the predatory look in his eyes. I could only guess at the kind of sick he is.

Naomi spent a week finding out.

"This time, I had no problem obliging." Desiree stares at me, drinking up the repulsion I'm not bothering to hide.

I'm stuck in place, wanting to run to Naomi's room to see for myself but not moving a muscle.

"You're lying," I say because I want it to be true.

Desiree tilts her head, her grin not letting up. "Why would I lie about that?"

She's right. I know she told him. He knew where I was. He knew my name.

He had Naomi.

Jesus, he had Naomi.

I swallow, my mouth painfully dry, and force myself to walk away, shaking Desiree off when she goes to grab my arm.

"FYI, if you think your fake master can protect you, you're wrong. This guy isn't afraid of Mr. A."

I keep walking, too intent on getting to Naomi to waste another breath on Desiree.

"While you're listening to your goth bitch friend's sob story, just remember, that's your future."

I halt in my tracks, my flip-flops squeaking on the tile. My jaw clenches, and I fist my hands at my sides.

Now *that* I can't let go.

I turn around and stomp toward Desiree. "What the *fuck* did you just call her?"

Desiree stays where she is while Lily steps to the side, her back pressing against the banister as I approach.

"You're kidding, right?" Desiree giggles. "You think goth bitch is bad? You should hear what all of us call *you*."

She must think I'm bluffing because her smile doesn't falter when I reach her. I shove her backward, watching her eyes widen and her smile fall in surprise.

"Don't you fucking talk about her!" I scream, stepping forward to push her again. She falls to the floor this time, and I climb on top of her. I growl and punch her face, once, twice, but when I rear back for a third swing, something stops my arm.

I turn my head to see Lily holding my arm like her life depends on it. Her eyes are wild, darting everywhere but me, and it takes a second to realize what she's looking for: a guard.

"Ahh!" Desiree bucks me off her and jerks up, grabbing my hair with Lily still holding my arm.

"You fucking whore!" Desiree screeches, ripping strands from my head. My scalp burns, but the surge of adrenaline that bursts through my bloodstream burns more.

I finally break Lily's hold and slash my nails in the direction of Desiree's face, hoping for contact with an eye.

"Stop!" Lily hisses in an angry whisper. As if whispering is necessary at this point. "Stop, both of you. You're going to get us into trouble."

Neither of us let up, and when I can't get to Desiree's skin, I find her hair and yank as forcefully as she yanks mine.

"What the hell is going on?"

Desiree's grip on my hair loosens at the sound of Sawyer's voice. We both ease up, but neither of us pull away entirely, not until someone wraps their arms around my waist and drags me back.

"Let go of me!" I shriek, thrashing against a man wearing too much cologne.

Sawyer hovers over Desiree with his jaw clenched. "*Get up*," he growls at her, nudging her with his shoe.

She stands, swatting matted blonde hair from her face as her glare lands on me.

"I know you're going to get away with this," Desiree sneers, her teeth bared. "But just know, Mr. A won't let me get hurt either."

"Are you serious right now?" Sawyer asks, his eyes wide with bewilderment. He slaps the back of her head, and she jerks forward, her eyes never leaving me.

"You're so goddamn obsessed with him, it's disgusting," I scoff. "Angel doesn't want you! Get the fuck over it!"

All at once, silence engulfs us. Four stunned faces look back at me, including Sawyer's, and my skin crawls as another second goes by.

"Angel?" Desiree asks, her voice small. "That's his name?"

"Goddamn it, get them out of here," Sawyer orders the guard at my back, the surprise on his face morphing into anger as he points at Desiree and Lily.

Desiree's anger returns as well, only worse now. Her face twists into a snarl, the only thing stopping her from looking feral is the lack of foam at her mouth. She throws an elbow back when the guard goes to grab her. "He told you his fucking name?!"

I don't answer.

I just fucked up. I know it, and I still don't quite care. So I just stare as Desiree is slung over the guard's shoulder—not without a fight—and carried off kicking and screaming. Lily scurries behind them with another guard at her back.

Now it's just me and Sawyer. I meet his eyes, then look down at the floor. My heart picks up its pace, and a sense of foreboding finally swallows me up.

"I'm sorry," I say before he can start in on me.

I find the courage to look at him as he blows out a breath, the anger leaving his expression with it.

"And you were doing so well." He shakes his head in disappointment. His voice is oddly calm. No yelling. No sneering.

"I'm sorry," I repeat because I'm not sure what else to do. "I didn't even think about saying his name. I was angry. Desiree, she—"

"Yeah, I'm going to be honest with you, I don't really give a shit what Desiree did or said. She's going to be gone soon anyway, so why don't you just save the fake apology?"

I frown with confusion.

He isn't angry.

Why isn't he angry?

"Just don't..." He searches for words and sighs. "You know what, fuck it. Scream Angel's name from the rooftops. I don't give a shit anymore." He throws up one hand like it truly doesn't matter to him, but I can see the defeat in his expression.

This doesn't make sense. This isn't Sawyer.

Another sigh, then he gestures down the hall behind me. "You should check on your friend."

I blink at him, standing in place a few more moments before I turn and start down the hall, half expecting him to shoot me in the back. After a few feet, my steps grow urgent, and my mind shifts away from everything that just happened and back to Naomi.

I throw open the door to her room and see her lying on the bed, facing away from me. I hurry over to the other side of the bed and drop to my knees.

Her eyes are open, and when she sees it's me, she gives me the smallest, saddest smile. "Should've known it was you making trouble out there."

I don't smile back.

My eyes are wide, and by the time I think to right myself, it's too late.

Both her eyes are puffy and bruised, and her jaw is painted various shades of purple and yellow. Her arm, partially hidden by the covers, is in a sling, and her neck is even more bruised than her face.

"Bad, I know," she rasps, her voice hoarse. She smiles like this is amusing, but there's too much sadness in her eyes to convince me.

I go along with the sarcasm anyway. I know Naomi well enough to understand it's how she copes.

"I don't know, I think this is actually an improvement."

She laughs then cringes, moving her other hand to her ribs. The blanket shifts with the movement, exposing bandages wrapped firmly around her midsection.

My eyes begin to burn. When Naomi notices, she moves her hand from her ribs, her teeth gritting.

"Don't cry, you weakling," she teases. "We said we were past that."

I choke on a laugh and cover my mouth, the bridge of my nose tingling with impending tears.

"What the hell were you doing out there?" she asks, probably trying to distract us both. "You woke me up."

"Sorry." I frown. "The cunt suddenly remembered I exist."

Naomi closes her puffy eyes, and I can tell by her pained expression that it hurts to keep them open. It probably hurts to move her eyelids at all.

"God, I hate her," Naomi snarls. "I hope one of these assholes smartens up and kills her."

"Don't say that."

"I mean it." Naomi cringes as she shifts, and I start to regret coming in here. For once, Desiree wasn't lying. Naomi needs her rest. "You should think so too after she tried to get you killed."

"I don't think like they do. I'm not a murderer... You shouldn't think like them either."

"If I could burn this whole island to the ground, I would. In a heartbeat. Even if you and I were still on it. *Fuck* them and everyone else here."

"Naomi..."

"What?" she snaps. This isn't the first time we've talked about things like this, but then I could tell she was joking. Now, I don't think she is.

"What did he do to you?" I whisper, my heart sinking to my stomach.

She winces, but not from physical pain this time.

Neither of us say anything for a long time, long enough that I give up on getting the answer I'm not sure I wanted to begin with.

A pained sound comes from Naomi, and it takes me a few moments to realize she's crying. If tears leak from her eyes, I can't see them with how beat up her face is. I cry tears for her, and getting as close as I can without hurting her, I put my hand on her back in a weak hug.

I close my eyes, silent tears sliding past my lids, and try not to make a sound. I try to be strong for her, which is what I know she would do for me. But it's a struggle. I've always been the weaker one.

"Promise me something," Naomi says, straining to quiet her sobs.

I open my eyes and look into brown irises pleading with me through two tiny slits.

"Promise me you won't let these fuckers fool you."

I stare at her as my chest seizes, forcing myself not to look away. I know exactly who and what she's referring to.

I wish I could explain it to her. I wish there was some way

she could possibly understand that Angel isn't like the man who did this to her. He wouldn't do this. He doesn't manipulate like Sawyer does or have the predatory nature of Jasper.

He's different. He's… He's not *them*.

But I can't tell her that. I know how it sounds. There's a part of me that still knows it could be a lie.

"I'll try," I say, lifting my lips into a sad smile.

She closes her eyes fully and holds her hand out for me. I hold onto it and let another tear escape.

"I'm tired." She sighs.

I clear my throat, hoping the turmoil that's drowning me won't be evident in my voice. "I'll let you get some rest."

"Lib." She tugs on my hand when I go to stand, and I crouch back down.

"Yeah?"

"Please don't leave me."

I give her hand a squeeze and try not to weep at how broken she sounds, how much vulnerability she just let leak through. "I'll stay… Get some rest."

Naomi hums but doesn't say anything else. I sit on the floor, still holding onto her hand as I rest my head against the bed.

I close my eyes, listening to Naomi's breaths until they become heavy. I hope her dreams are better than her reality.

Maybe she'll have a few hours of peace.

ANGEL

I drum my fingers on Sawyer's desk while staring at the monitor showing the playroom. The cameras in there are infrared, so I can see better on the monitor than I could from actually being in there. But also, I'm avoiding being around Lib while she dances for other men.

My eyes travel to the cage she's perched in, the compulsion too strong. She's much better at avoiding me than I am at avoiding her.

Lib hasn't spoken to me in four days. Ever since Naomi returned from Jasper's house, things have been different. I'm at the manor nearly all day while Sawyer is gone, and she's managed to see me less than when I'm working from home.

It worried me at first, hearing, "yes sir," and, "no sir," watching her excuse herself any time I walked into a room, getting a brush off every time I tried to ask what was wrong. I thought for sure she'd somehow found out things about me that pushed her away for good, but I don't think it's that anymore. She isn't showing any anger or fear toward me. It's only avoidance.

So it's Naomi. It has to be. Does Lib feel guilty for some

reason? Is she refusing to speak to me because I make her life the slightest bit more comfortable than the others?

I should've never allowed Jasper to take the girl.

A knock sounds on the door, and I pull my eyes from the screen in time to see Jasper entering the office.

Speak of the devil.

I go back to the screen, ignoring the smirk that raises one side of his lips.

"Not partaking in the fun?" he asks, shutting the door behind him before coming to sit in a chair in front of the desk.

I lean back in my chair and shake my head, forcing my hardened gaze to him. "I don't much care for the playroom."

He nods knowingly. "You're more into Chaffer's parties, aren't you?"

He's lived on the island for a few weeks. How could he already know what I'm into?

Oh, right, this is Jasper.

"Yes."

His smirk lifts. "Me too. Sawyer's tastes are too over the top."

"Mmm." I slowly nod. "And yet you've been in the playroom almost every night since you arrived on the island."

He shrugs. "I don't have a slave yet. Once I do, I'm sure I'll join you at Chaffer's." His lip twitches. "You haven't been lately, though, have you?"

"Work," I deadpan.

"Right."

We stare at each other, letting the silent challenge hang in the air, clinging to my skin like moisture. There's so much depravity in his eyes, it could make a grown man squirm, and if I'm being honest, sometimes I have a difficult time looking.

I wasn't quite honest with Lib about who Jasper is. He's a

friend … in a way. I've known him since college. Our senior year, Sawyer, Jasper, and I even rented a house together. But Jasper doesn't get close enough to be anyone's genuine friend, and even if he let someone in on whatever's happening in that fucked-up mind of his, no one would be brave enough to look.

What Jasper is to me is a tool. Now and back then. His depravity has proven useful in certain circumstances.

"Speaking of slaves," he says, leaning back and interlacing his fingers behind his neck. "I think I've found the one I want."

"Is that so?"

A smirk plays on his lips. "Uh huh. I was planning on buying her the other night, but Sawyer says you've already claimed her. How does that work exactly?"

My fingers curl into taut fists. "What do you mean?"

"I *mean*, how could you have claimed her if she's still here at the manor shaking her sexy ass for residents? Wouldn't that make her up for grabs?"

My eyes widen at his brazenness, and my jaw clenches. I take my time responding, choosing each word carefully.

"*No.*" I take a breath to ensure my next words are steady. "Sawyer and I have an arrangement. Since I'm not allowed my own slave, Ivy is as close as it gets for me. She isn't for sale."

"Mm." His lips twist to one side while he pretends to consider this. "Is she allowed to be borrowed?"

"Like the other girl you decided to *borrow*?" I clasp my hands together so I don't reach across the desk and strangle him. "No."

He fights a smile. "Are you miffed about that too? I thought it was just Sawyer."

"You beat the shit out of her, Jasper. Everyone has their limits."

He barks out a laugh. "Should I remember that the next time you have a job for me to do?"

He waits like it's a real question, but I don't answer. The truth is, I'd rather not know the methods he uses to complete the jobs Sawyer and I give him. He handles a lot of our dirty work when twenty-first century civility isn't an effective business tactic. Some of that dirty work involves hearts stopping. My imagination provides me plenty.

"Besides," he goes on, his posture far too relaxed, "how was I supposed to know how you and Sawyer run things around here? I thought the girl's escape attempt warranted harsher punishment than… How did you punish the brunette exactly? I'm still not clear on that."

Again, I don't answer. He's full of shit, and he knows I know it. He claims Naomi tried to run away, and I believe it, but I also believe he gave her good reason to. She wasn't trying to run from the island, she was trying to run from him. There's a difference.

As for how I chose to punish Lib, I'm sure Sawyer has already told Jasper plenty.

"Ivy."

One of his brows slants. "Hmm?"

"Her name is Ivy."

"Ah." He rests his hands on his stomach, his head slowly rising and falling as if this is truly new information. "Yes, Ivy. How did you handle the situation with her?"

"There was no situation. I chose to force her to make a call. She did nothing wrong."

He smiles yet again, staring at me like I'm a child showing him a clumsy juggling act. He knows I'm lying… I didn't expect anything different. He's better at reading people than anyone I've ever met. I'm still not going to admit the truth.

I clear my throat. "If Sawyer still plans on allowing you to have your own slave, you should start looking for someone else. I don't anticipate being done with Ivy any time soon."

"If he plans on *allowing* me?" Jasper tilts his head.

Oh, right. How dare someone tell him what he can or cannot do? I struggle not to roll my eyes, but it does occur to me that he and I are similar in some ways.

"It is his island, after all."

"And yet here you are, bending his rules," he says, splaying his hands. "I've always liked that about you, though. You command what you want instead of relying on manipulation tactics like Sawyer." He pulls his hands in front of him and leans forward. "Between you and me, I think he's the soft one."

"I'd say you're as equally talented at manipulating Sawyer as he is anyone else, considering you still manage to come here."

"No." His arrogant smile gradually deadens. "I don't need guile. I much prefer taking what I want with force."

I nearly snort at the veiled threat.

Try me, motherfucker.

"You can try." One side of my lips lift. "Brawn can only accomplish so much."

"It's usually enough."

When my smirk falls, he pushes himself out of the chair. "Well, guess I'll get back in there. Just wanted to see how my oldest mate was doing. It must get lonely, staring wistfully at a monitor." He winks and turns toward the door.

"Jasper?"

He looks over his shoulder. "Hmm?"

"We don't allow guests to provide their names to the manor whores."

"Right." He taps his forehead. "Sorry, boss man. Won't happen again."

He faces forward and leaves. As soon as he's gone, my lungs expand, and the room doesn't seem as small.

I close my eyes and roll the tension from my neck, trying not to allow Jasper's challenging tone to get to me. If there's one person I wouldn't want to get into a war with, it's him. I would tear apart everything he's built for himself. He would skin anyone I've ever loved alive. Neither of us would come out intact.

When I open my eyes and look at the screen, I'm not surprised to see Jasper making his way through the playroom toward Lib. When he gets to the edge of the stage, he looks up, searching for a camera. Once he finds it, his lips spread into a wide smile, and he gives a little wave. I'm reminded of another commonality between us.

Once we decide we want something, we don't let up.

LIBERTY

TWO DAYS LATER

*M*y heart beats to the rhythm of the staccato music blaring in my ears as I make my way from the playroom. I can feel eyes on my back, but I don't turn around, too afraid to see Jasper following me.

He's been playing this cat and mouse game for days, and I wish I would stop letting him. I've been darting upstairs as soon as my shifts end to check on Naomi, but I've been running away from Jasper as much as I've been running toward her.

He scares the shit out of me. All he makes are subtle comments, but his eyes alone are enough to make my skin crawl. Tonight, he isn't the only one I'm running from, though.

I've met Angel's eyes multiple times this evening, watching me from the bar. I suspect he's been waiting for me to leave as well. It takes more willpower than should be necessary to keep myself from running into his arms for protection.

I want to be done with it. With *him*. I started off feeling like playing the damsel and knight game was a betrayal to

Naomi, but the more days that go by, the more I realize it's a betrayal to myself.

This thing between us has to stop. I can't be his surrogate slave, and I'm ashamed for ever wanting to be.

Cooper opens the door when I get near, and I hear Angel calling my name. A brief moment of relief that it isn't Jasper pulls a rush of air from my lungs as I leave the playroom, ignoring Angel.

"Jesus, Liberty, would you just talk to me?" Angel asks, stepping into the hallway. The door shuts, and it's only the two of us, but I keep walking. I fully expect him to follow, maybe even physically force me to stop, but footsteps don't sound behind me.

I throw a look over my shoulder and get another burst of relief when there's no one there. I turn down another hallway and stop, flattening my back against the wall and breathing for a minute.

I close my eyes and try to get the image of Jasper winking at me this evening out of my mind, try to stop picturing everything he did to Naomi, try to forget the sounds of her screaming out in the middle of the night.

I pull in a deep breath and open my eyes, pushing off the wall and heading for the kitchen. My stomach rumbles just thinking about food. I lose my appetite every night before heading into the playroom, but I'm starving by the time I leave.

Hunger gnaws more with each step I take away from Angel and Jasper. When I push through the swinging doors and step into the kitchen, no one at my back, I let out a sigh, massaging my temples with two fingers.

"Rough night?"

My shoulders lift, tensing like a wet cat, and I jump away from the voice, knocking into the doors that boomerang into my back.

My hand flies to my chest, and I sigh when I see it's just Sawyer leaning against the kitchen counter.

Just Sawyer. See what my life has become?

One side of his lips lifts as he nods behind me. "Which one are you running from? Jasper or Angel?"

"Both," I answer honestly, walking to the kitchen island and leaning my elbows on the granite. Adrenaline drains from me, taking my energy with it. "I didn't know you were back."

"I got in this evening."

"Oh." Silence fills the space, but somehow, it isn't awkward. This tiny exchange is the most civil we've been.

"You're awfully popular with the psychopaths." Sawyer pushes off the counter and comes to stand across from me. "I almost feel bad for you."

"Almost." I smile with morbid amusement.

More silence.

"How's April doing?"

My jaw tightens, and I stare down at the granite. I get the immediate urge to correct him on Naomi's name, but that isn't what has the blood rushing to my ears.

How fucking *dare* he ask about Naomi.

I'm about to push off the island and walk from the kitchen, but Sawyer's voice halts me.

"I'm sorry about what happened," he says, guilt choking his words.

I look up at him but don't say anything.

"Jasper is…" He runs a hand through his hair and sighs. "Fuck, I don't even know. I didn't realize he would go that far."

My eyes narrow, but the urge to fight Sawyer isn't as strong as it used to be. "He said she tried to run. Isn't that punishable by death by your standards?"

And aren't you the guy who wanted to fuck and kill me simultaneously?

He frowns and doesn't respond to that. The way he looks at me makes me think I'm missing something. Or that he thinks I'm missing something.

"He lied about it," I add, just so he's aware I'm not a moron. And also because I'm not quite convinced he knows the truth. "Nao— ... *April* told me what happened. The twisted piece of shit tortured her for a week, and when he was done, he cut her loose and *told* her to run. It was a game to him. He only wanted—"

"Thank you, Ivy. I'm aware."

I close my mouth and squint at him, waiting for him to explain.

Another sigh. Another hand through his hair. "I told you the day you arrived here; some residents have dark tastes. Jasper is one of those residents. I just didn't... I..." He pauses while searching for words. "I didn't think he would go that far. I wouldn't have allowed him to borrow her if I'd known."

He closes his eyes and shakes his head. "I should've listened to Angel."

My lungs seem to shrink. "What?"

Sawyer's eyes open, and he studies my face for several moments. I can tell the moment he decides not to respond because he breaks eye contact and stretches his arms, a move people make right before they decide it's time to leave.

"Angel knew Jasper had April, didn't he?" I ask, already knowing it's true. It shrinks my lungs even more, but I'm not surprised. Especially considering he and Jasper are ... friends. I guess.

I'm not shocked that Angel would lie to me ... but it still hurts.

When Sawyer doesn't say anything, I lean my head back and roll my neck.

"You and I have shitty taste in friends."

I open my eyes and glare at him.

He chuckles, but it contains little humor. "I'm not wrong."

"You're so much worse than Angel," I say, unjustified protectiveness flaring.

He smiles, and it's almost … sad. "You think so?"

"I know so."

He laughs again, shaking his head. "You don't know Angel, sweetheart… You will, though. Keep rejecting him like you have been, and you'll find out who he is sooner rather than later."

My mind searches for a retort, but the look on Sawyer's face muddies my thoughts. He isn't amused. He doesn't sound or look like he's forcing seriousness. He's … well, he's bothered by something. This is the most vulnerable I've seen him.

"He told you I was rejecting him?" I ask, fear working its way in. Fear of who? Of Angel? That's a weird twist.

Sawyer shrugs. "He said you won't talk to him. I'm curious, is it because you're pissed about April? Because in his defense, he was against Jasper taking her. He's been trying to convince Jasper to buy Desiree. But of course," he laughs dryly and waves his hand toward me, "Jasper only wants you."

The hairs raise on the back of my neck, and a lump clogs my throat. None of what Sawyer's saying is surprising, but it's terrifying to hear the words spoken aloud.

"Angel wants impossible things," I force the words past the lump, my voice soft.

Sawyer nods. "That's typical of him."

"I'm not angry with him or trying to reject him, I just … don't think I can be who he wants me to be."

Sawyer smiles compassionately, which only makes this

exchange stranger. "You and I have more in common than you realize."

I blink at him, unable to say any more with my throat closing.

He's a master manipulator, I remind myself. *This is the mask he's chosen to show you before, as saltyshells.*

Sawyer slaps the table and turns. "You know what, you and I could use a drink." He walks to the wine rack to grab a bottle and two glasses that dangle from a holder.

He sets everything down on the granite island, then turns, hesitating like he's forgotten something. When he remembers whatever it is, he walks to a drawer and sifts through it before pulling out a corkscrew. My eyes move to the bottle.

Cabernet.

I can't place when the churning in my gut starts, but one moment I'm focused on the clog in my throat, and the next, it's out of my mind. I stare at the bottle until my eyes become dry.

I blink several times, trying to clear my vision as Sawyer removes the cork and fills the glasses.

My heart cracks, and pathetic, sad tears well in my eyes. He scoots mine toward me, red wine sloshing onto the counter when his movement falters. I keep my gaze on the glass instead of meeting his eyes, but I can tell the moment he notices something's wrong.

The air dissipates from the room.

Don't cry.

It's just a lapse in judgment. It means nothing.

Sawyer is a predator. He talks to so many women, he couldn't possibly remember everything about me. It makes sense he wouldn't remember that I don't drink wine.

Everything Sawyer and I had was fake. It was just an act. None of it matters.

Don't you fucking cry, Lib.

"What's wrong?" Sawyer asks, his tone laced with concern.

I close my eyes and shake my head.

"If you're worried about Jasper, don't be. I'm not allowing him to take home any more slaves until he purchases one, and it won't be you. You can relax."

My breath stutters. "It isn't that."

I meet Sawyer's soft blue eyes and picture him as the man I almost fell in love with. The man I thought was my one reprieve from my shitty-ass life.

He looks so handsome, so *innocent* with his wavy blond hair and stretched T-shirt. It feels impossible for this man to be both the monster I've come to know and the man I thought I knew better than anyone.

He frowns. "What is it then?"

I motion to the glass. "I can't drink this. I have a wine allergy."

Sawyer purses his lips like he's confused, plunging the knife deeper into my chest.

Why? Why do I let this bother me?

"O-kay?" Sawyer drawls. "I can get you something else?"

"You really don't remember me at all, do you?" I ask, holding back the floodgates. All those nights, wasted. All the trust, the friendship, the *longing* was all one-sided. And for what?

Anger starts to mix with sadness as I look down at the island, hoping that avoiding his eyes will make it easier to say the words I've been dying to say since I found out who Sawyer was. "Was it really necessary to spend so much time making me think I was falling in love with you? Did you really need to..." I clear my throat. "My husband sold me to you. What possible benefit could you have had for doing that?"

"What are you talking about?"

I look up to find Sawyer's eyes narrowed in confusion.

"The chat site," I say, more anger brewing at his bewilderment.

Recognition flares, and he sighs like he's relieved. "Oh." He chuckles, pushing a fallen lock off his forehead. "Yeah, that wasn't me."

My jaw relaxes, and I stare at him with even more confusion than he showed me.

"I led you to believe I was your internet boyfriend because I didn't want you to suspect your husband had anything to do with you being here."

My mouth opens and closes several times before I can speak. "I don't understand."

Sawyer's head tilts. "What's so confusing about it?"

"If it wasn't you I was talking to, who was it?"

He shrugs. "I don't know."

"What do you mean you don't know?" I ask, beginning to feel exasperated.

"I *mean*, as far as I'm aware, you weren't catfished. That was just some guy. Your husband found out about your internet fling and got pissed, which is why you're here."

I blink several times. Sawyer speaks so matter-of-factly, but none of this makes sense. "But you knew my screen name."

"Because Robert told me. What was it again?" His eyes flicker back and forth as he searches his mind, snapping his fingers when it comes to him. "Manhattan peasant. Not sure how that's fitting, but it's cute."

My head swims as I continue trying to make sense of this. In a way, this helps. I feel less betrayed by the man I thought I was falling in love with and less stupid being around Sawyer. I also feel more anger toward the man I married.

But there's one other man in this mess, and I don't know how to feel about him. Angel lied to me.

Again.

But why?

The obvious answer flashes in my mind, but I shove it away, unable to accept it yet.

"Did Robert show you the transcripts?" I ask.

Sawyer's brow lifts above his glass as he takes a sip. "What?"

"From my messages with saltyshells. Did Robert show you our exchanges?"

"You think he carried around copies of your internet affair?" He laughs. "What?"

"Just answer the question."

"*No*, Ivy. I didn't read anything. He just told me about it."

"Did Angel read any?"

Sawyer looks at his glass as he swirls its contents. "Why are you freaking out about this?"

"*Sawyer*," I grind out. "Did Angel see any of my messages?"

Setting his glass down, he props his forearms on the table with just enough force to show his frustration. "Why would he?"

Why would he?

Good question.

I think about the Manhattan Angel ordered me and the chocolates he brought back from his business trip, the way he thought it was ridiculous for me to think he read so much of my exchanges with saltyshells.

He was right, it would've been ridiculous. He didn't read them.

He wrote them.

"Did Robert tell you and Angel anything else about me?" I ask, still grasping at the possibility that my gut is wrong.

"Like?"

"Did he mention my favorite drink? Or my favorite chocolate or anything like that? Did..." I clear my throat and close my eyes for a moment, remembering all the long talks I had with saltyshells. All the intimate details of my life I shared.

"Sawyer, is Angel saltyshells?"

Sawyer laughs incredulously. "What? No. Why would you…?"

I watch as Sawyer weighs the possibility. Suddenly, he doesn't seem so sure.

I turn and stride from the kitchen, my stomach twisting into knots but no longer from hunger. I walk and walk and walk, unsure of my destination, just knowing I need to continue.

It makes so much sense now that I hate myself for not seeing it. I hate myself for not seeing through his bullshit.

This is why Angel has been interested in me from the beginning. *This* is why he hasn't let up. *This* is why he's been happy to play the part of knight in shining armor.

He hasn't wanted me since I got here.

He's wanted me for over a year.

But why?

Why?

Why?

Why?

And how? How did he find me through the chat site? Why did he care to look in the first place?

So many whys.

So many unknowns.

I think I'm going to puke.

I run to a balcony on the third floor, flinging open the doors that lead to it. I rush to the ledge and grasp the railing, seesawing air in and out of my lungs, trying to calm the nausea.

It doesn't work.

I spin around and move a couple feet toward a potted

plant before falling to my knees. I hurl bile into the pot, the clay rim sanding away at my fingertips. I dry heave long after my stomach is empty and saliva hangs from my lip.

Tears blur my vision, and my nose begins to run. They aren't sad tears. They aren't even betrayed tears.

They're angry tears. Anger toward myself. Anger for trying so hard to keep my promise to Naomi yet failing miserably.

Don't let these bastards fool me?

This one takes the cake.

I let out a scream, gripping the planter so hard my fingers hurt. I stand up, yanking the pot up with me. I slam it to the ground with another guttural scream, sending shards of clay flying on the balcony and vomit-covered soil spreading across the stone.

"Trouble in paradise?"

I turn and face Desiree with her hip popped out and a smug smile lifting her lips.

She raises a perfectly curved eyebrow. "Seriously, what the hell crawled up *your* ass?"

I laugh pitifully and take a step toward her. "I *wish* I could tell you what a fucking idiot you are, Desiree, but I don't think words can define it."

I stand inches from her, my hands balled into fists at my sides. I don't know if this is a long time coming or if Desiree is just in the wrong place at the wrong time, but all the rage I feel directs toward her like a heat-seeking missile.

"You've really convinced yourself that you want Angel. Well, please, *please* take him." I shove her shoulder, forcing her to back up a step.

Another laugh barrels out of me, and I must look manic because her usual look of disdain is replaced by uneasy bewilderment. "He wants the psychopath to buy you, you idiot! *That's* what you mean to him. You know, the same guy you thought was hilarious for beating up Naomi? Yeah, Angel wants him to take you. He fucking *hates* you!"

I shove her again, and she stumbles, her eyes widening.

She recovers a moment later, her face pinched with the same rage I'm feeling. I realize now that *this* is what I wanted. Company in my betrayal. Hatred for the same man who fooled me. A fight. Hell, a fucking brawl. Anything but me pathetically puking into a potted plant.

"You're a lying fucking bitch!" she seethes, lunging for me so quickly, I don't realize she's coming until her palms hit my chest.

I stagger back a few steps, then my teeth bare as I growl. I launch myself at her, but she puts her hands up to block me.

She slaps me across the face, and my head whips to the side. I don't have time to react before she clutches my hair, reminiscent of the first time we fought, and yanks with so much force that I yelp. The scream that comes from her next drowns out my protest.

She throws me against the railing and uses her whole body to trap me against it as she squeezes my throat with both of her hands. Her wild eyes bore into me with so much rage that it actually sobers me for a moment.

She's even more pissed than I am.

I snap out of my surprise and claw at her hands, but they're too tight. I scratch her face, giving her a warning before I gouge out her eyes. My nails leave dotted lines of blood on her cheeks, and her grip on me loosens, gifting me with a burst of oxygen. I push her away from me with a growl before she jerks a knee up, connecting with my stomach.

What little air I have leaves my lungs, and a new round of nausea takes hold. When I double over, she takes the opportunity to crash her knee into my face.

Pain explodes through my nose, and for a moment, it's

the only part of my body my brain registers. Blood streams down over my lips as I release a roar.

"I hate you!" Desiree screams, drilling her elbow between my shoulder blades.

More pain. More screams.

More adrenaline.

I lift up and flail my fists toward her, but she's already there with a punch to my face. Her hits push me closer to the ledge until my back bounces against it.

I land a blow to her jaw and send her stumbling. Panting with pain radiating from every inch of my body, I grab hold of her wrist before she can recover, and I jerk her toward me with as much force as my body will allow. I twist out of the way so I don't ram her into myself, my hand still yanking, momentum building, my teeth still bared, still seeing red.

I only mean to slam her into the railing. I only mean to get the upper hand.

But that isn't what happens.

My eyes widen, and my jaw goes slack when I register that Desiree's weight is tipping her over the ledge. All my anger drains from my face along with my blood, and in a panic, I tighten my grip on her wrist to bring her back.

Her momentum jerks her from my grasp, and her body soars, flying horizontally for a couple feet, her body twisting, her legs kicking, finding nothing but air.

Time moves slowly. Slowly enough that I can see the fear on her face, hear the terror in her scream, make out the way her skirt flaps as she barrels toward the ground. I stand frozen, leaned over the railing with my hand extended.

A scream pierces my ears, and it isn't until Desiree's body hits the ground, her limbs twisting awkwardly, that I realize it's my own scream I'm hearing.

I stare at Desiree, my eyes white saucers in my skull. I hear a yell followed by pounding footsteps below. A man drops to his knees in front of her body before looking up at me.

But I don't move. I don't blink.

It isn't until I sense someone at my back that I remember to worry about my own life instead of the dead woman on the ground. The one I killed.

Another yell.

Another scream.

My heart pounds harder than it ever has. Fear claws at me, mixing with regret I didn't know possible, and I find myself hoping for things I swore I wouldn't. Hoping for a savior. A knight.

An angel.

I find myself preparing to play the damsel in distress.

Just one more time.

To be continued…

* * *

Ack, talk about a cliffhanger! I hope you enjoyed this first installment! If you'd like to continue on this wild journey with Angel and Liberty, you can do so in book two, <u>TAMING LIBERTY ;)</u>

THANK YOU

Thank you so much for your interest in *Caging Liberty*! This one is so special to me because it captures so many firsts. The largest being my first trilogy.

This story would never have fit into one book (I can't even imagine trying), but I was nervous about keeping so many things straight across so many pages or running out of things to say. It was something I anticipated being a great challenge, but I enlisted my fabulous editor, Kim Bookjunkie, for help with my first worry, and for my second, what I found was, I'm actually incredibly wordy and could've went on forever (surprised LOL?). So after this, I'm sure you can expect more trilogies! The only thing I hated was writing the cliffhangers because they make me feel guilty, but I'm confident you'll forgive me.

I really hope you enjoyed reading about Angel and Liberty. If you did, please consider leaving a review or shooting me an email. I love hearing what readers have to say <3

Oh, and sign up for my newsletter at nicolecypher.com

for my FREE bully romance, Vicious Knight, as well as exclusive bonus chapters and updates on upcoming novels and giveaways.

With love, always,
Nicole

Vicious Knight

Everyone has secrets...

What do you do to the person who learns yours?

I'll tell you what I did. I went after her.

I **wrecked** her credibility.

I **destroyed** her friendships.

I **ruined** her reputation.

And she responded in the most foolish way possible. She fought back.

My last name might be Knight, but she's the furthest thing from being rescued.

This book contains scenes and situations that may be triggering for some. Reader discretion is advised.

ALSO BY NICOLE CYPHER

For a comprehensive list, check out Nicole's website

The Darker Places Series:

DESIRED

DEPLORABLE

DETHRONED

DEMOLISHED

JULIUS

Soulless Kings MC:

FENDER

JOKER

Gruco Crime Family Series:

HIS PROMISE

HIS PET

HIS PRIZE

HIS PUPPET

HIS PROPERTY

HIS PASSEROTTA (Coming December 2023!)

Liberating Deceit:

CAGING LIBERTY

TAMING LIBERTY

CLAIMING LIBERTY

Standalone Novels:

UNHINGED

VICIOUS KNIGHT

ABOUT THE AUTHOR

Nicole Cypher is an author and avid reader of dark romance. She began her writing journey in college and hasn't looked back since. In her books you can expect a yummy anti-hero, plenty of action, and a happy ending.

Be sure to sign up for her newsletter at nicolecypher.com to stay up to date on the latest releases, special offers, and exclusive bonus chapters.

BB

www.ingramcontent.com/pod-product-compliance
Lightning Source LLC
Chambersburg PA
CBHW020911160726
47993CB00005B/1919